P9-DNB-506

 Published by Arthur A. Levine Books, an imprint of Scholastic Inc., *Publishers since 1920*, by arrangement with Ediciones SM, Madrid, Spain.

The author has revised the original Spanish text for its English-language publication.

Library of Congress Cataloging-in-Publication Data

Gallego García, Laura, 1977– [Valle de los lobos. English]

The Valley of the Wolves / by Laura Gallego García; translated by Margaret Sayers Peden.

—1st ed. p. cm.

Summary: Chosen to study at an academy of high sorcery known as the Tower, ten-year-old Dana finds herself, as her apprenticeship in magic progresses, growing increasingly curious about the history of the Tower and the true nature of her invisible best friend Kai.

ISBN 0-439-58553-8

[1. Magic—Fiction. 2. Wizards—Fiction. 3. Best friends—Fiction. 4. Friendship—Fiction. 5. Ghosts—Fiction.] I. Peden, Margaret Sayers. II. Title.

PZ7.G155625Val 2006 [Fic]Mdc22 2005029987

10 9 8 7 6 5 4 3 2 1 06 07 08 09 10

Printed in the United States of America 37

First edition, April 2006

The Valley

BY LAURA GALLEGO GARCÍA

of the

TRANSLATED BY MARGARET SAYERS PEDEN

ARTHUR A. LEVINE BOOKS

An Imprint of Scholastic Inc.

For Jack, the authentic Kai

-L.G.G.

Love is the one bridge
between the visible and the invisible
that everyone knows.

Do not concern yourself
with explaining emotions.
Live intensely
and hold what you have felt
to be a gift from God.
If you believe that you cannot survive
in a world where it is more important
to live than to understand,
then give up magic.

You will never be mine,
and that is why I will have you always.

— Paulo Coelho, *Brida*

Contents

1 Kai

A fierce wind whipped the branches of the trees and furiously shook the bushes and grass. Its terrible voice roared across the grange. There was no moon in the cloudless sky, and not a light shone in the wild night.

The farm buildings bore the blasts heroically, creaking only under the most furious assaults, and the inhabitants of the house slept tranquilly. There had been many other nights like this in their inhospitable land, and they knew the roof was not going to collapse upon their heads. The animals stirred in the barn, however — perhaps roused by more than the terrible storm.

As the walls of the house moaned in protest against the force of the wind, a sudden scream pierced the night, waking the entire grange. Moments later a young boy raced from the house on an urgent mission: He had to bring back the midwife as soon as possible.

In the terrified household, confusion reigned. The baby was not due for two more months, but the mother's labor pains had already started, and their intensity frightened her. She had brought five children into the world already and never suffered so much. Now she lay struggling, and the other members of the family feared for both mother and child.

A while later, puffing and panting, the boy and the midwife arrived. The father and other children were crowded anxiously around the bed. "Everyone out!" the old woman cried as she hobbled forward. The family scrambled out of the room, closing the door behind them.

Outside the door, they waited and waited. The time seemed to stretch endlessly. The wind raised its pitch, and rain began to pelt the land and the buildings. At last another cry shattered the night, challenging the roar outside.

"My child!" the father shouted exultantly and rushed into the room. His wife lay on the bed, exhausted and sweating, but still alive. The midwife stood at her side, cradling a bawling little creature in her arms. But the expression on her face stopped the father in his tracks.

"What is it?" he asked. "Isn't she healthy?"

"Your daughter is fine," the old woman hastened to assure him.

She was a tiny, wrinkled baby girl with dark blue eyes. One lock of black hair adorned a head that seemed too large for her body. She looked like a normal newborn in every way.

But the midwife never told anyone about the sparks she had seen deep in those sapphire eyes.

They named her Dana, and she grew up as just another child among many brothers and sisters. Since the survival of the family depended on the cooperation of all its members, the little girl soon understood her place in the family and the importance of her responsibilities around the farm: feed the chickens, wash the dishes, weed the vegetables, and care for her youngest sisters. She was a quick learner and performed her chores diligently, without protest.

Her parents never treated her in any special way, and yet everyone could tell that she was different from her brothers and sisters. They saw it in her inward nature and her grave, pensive gaze. She preferred to play alone, and seldom spoke or smiled.

And then she met Kai.

It was the year Dana was six years old, on an especially warm summer's day. She had risen early in order to finish her work before the sun reached its highest point. Having fed the chickens, she was gathering raspberries to make jam when she felt someone behind her.

"Hello," a boy's voice said.

Dana turned. A smiling boy was sitting on the rock wall that separated the barn enclosure from the raspberry bushes, watching her pick the sticky fruit. Though he was about her age, Dana had never seen him before; but her family tended to keep to themselves, so that was not unusual. He was skinny, with unruly blond hair that fell to his shoulders, and his green eyes shone in a friendly fashion. Even so, she did not reply to his greeting but merely returned to her berry picking.

"My name is Kai," the boy said to her back.

Dana turned again, surprised. Who was this boy? Why was he speaking to her as if he had known her all his life? What was he looking for? After another quick glance, however, she saw nothing in his face except friendly sincerity. His green eyes were focused on her, and there was something in them. . . . An invitation? Dana had the impression that those eyes were filled with promises, and suddenly she felt that she wanted to go forward and meet them. For once in her life, she let herself be led by her instinct, and she burst through the barrier that separated her from the rest of the world.

"I am Dana." And then she smiled too.

At first they didn't see each other very often. Kai seemed to come to the grange only when she was alone; he would find her hidden away from her family and they would talk endlessly. He longed to see distant lands and live great adventures. He knew countless stories about remote times; about when dragons roamed the world; about the days when the lands of elves — which, according to what he told her, lay on both sides of the ocean — had not seemed to be so far; about when there were wise and good sorcerers, and powerful heroes who did battle armed with magical, legendary swords. Dana listened to all these stories wide-eyed. Kai's tales opened her imagination to a world that she would scarcely have dared to dream about before she met him. In her house, stories about fabulous beings and places were not greatly appreciated; after all, if such things did exist, they were too far away ever to affect the life of her family, and therefore did not warrant thinking about. Nevertheless, Dana learned to be an avid listener, drinking in the stories Kai told, her eyes dreamy, as both contemplated the cottony clouds streaking the sky.

Soon Kai began to show up every day. He would appear early in the morning to help Dana with her chores — he was especially good with the animals — then they would run off, laughing, into the forest. Together they whistled to birds, tracked deer, climbed the highest trees, and explored the most hidden, wild corners of the woods.

The forest had no secrets from Kai. If Dana had thought she knew the world around her, she realized how mistaken she was the day he stopped her from eating some delicious-looking berries.

"Don't touch that!" he exclaimed when she was about to pull the berry from the bush. Dana's hand froze in midair.

"Why? What is it?"

Kai did not answer. He pointed to something at Dana's feet. A little "Oh!" escaped her when she saw what it was.

On the ground, half-hidden in the grass, lay the body of a squirrel. It still held a half-eaten red berry between its paws. Dana drew her hand back and looked at Kai with a new respect. He immediately smiled, though a spark of worry still shone in his green eyes.

From that moment on, Dana liked him still more.

A few days later, they were chatting in the stable as they fed the horses, when they were surprised by Dana's mother and one of her older sisters returning from the fields.

"Who are you talking to, Dana?" her mother asked.

"To Kai," she replied and turned to introduce her friend. To her bewilderment, he wasn't there.

"Who is Kai?"

Only then did Dana realize that in all the time she had known Kai, she had never told her family about him.

"He's my friend," she answered quickly. "Kai," she called, whirling around, but there was no sign of him. "He was here just a minute ago!" she cried when she saw her mother's exasperated expression.

Her mother shook her head, and her sister laughed. Dana wanted to explain but she couldn't find the words; she stood staring as the two women left the stable and headed toward the house.

For the rest of the morning she looked for Kai, planning to scold him for having left so suddenly, but he was nowhere to be found. She waited all afternoon for him to come back; *but even if he does show up, I won't speak to him*, she decided eventually.

The next day, Dana left the house early as usual to collect eggs. Kai was sitting on the rock wall as usual, a happy smile on his lips.

She walked past him without a glance and went straight to the chicken coop.

"What's the matter?" he asked as he followed her. "Are you angry at me?"

Dana hung the basket on her arm and began to gather eggs.

Kai looked at her for a moment, then he too began to shift the chickens aside and collect the warm eggs from their nests. Dana had always enjoyed these times together among the quiet clucks of the hens, the buzzing of a few insects, the soft shadows and sharp smell of the coop in the early morning, but for the first time she found herself wondering whether Kai didn't have a farm where he had to help out, or parents who assigned him chores he had to do.

"I'm sorry, Dana," Kai whispered in her ear.

"You just vanished!" she cried. "My mother and sister thought I was lying!"

"I'm sorry," he said again, his tone sincere.

"Why did you do that?"

"I thought it was for the best."

"But why?"

Kai shifted uncomfortably.

"Don't you want to meet my family?" Dana asked.

"It isn't that. It's just . . . it would be best if you don't talk to them about me. If they don't know I'm here."

"But I don't understand!" What *did* she know about him, really? Nothing! What if he was a thief, or something worse? "Where do you live?" she asked suddenly. "Do your parents mind that you come here all the time?"

"No . . ." he said slowly. "They don't mind." He looked into her eyes. "Please trust me, Dana. It's much better if your family doesn't know anything about me. Better for both of us. Someday I'll explain, but not right now. Just don't talk about me. Will you do that?"

Dana nodded, but in her heart, a little flame of doubt began to flicker.

The seasons raced by, and they both grew taller and stronger. At eight, Kai was no longer a skinny little kid but a healthy, well-built boy, while Dana's curly hair, black as a crow's wing, reached down her back to her slender waist. They still spent most of their time together. Occasionally she tried to ask him who he was, where he came from, but he would give evasive answers or change the subject. And Dana learned that, although Kai's friendship seemed unconditional, there was a line she was not allowed to cross, a line that was not limited only to questions he did not want to answer. Once when they were walking together, she reached out to take his hand in hers. He snatched it away as if she'd tried to pinch him. "What do you think you're doing?"

"I'm sorry," Dana said in confusion. Maybe she had gone too far; maybe there was a boundary for familiarity between a boy and a girl. She was already aware that her friend always shrank from physical contact with her, although she had never before seen him demonstrate that so brusquely. After a moment, he smiled, and Dana relaxed; but she knew intuitively that however closely their souls might be united, a perplexing abyss lay between them.

One gray, cloudy day after doing the chores, Dana and Kai ran to the forest. They followed a deer, then watched twin bear cubs loping along through the underbrush after their mother. They filled up on wild blackberries and turned over rocks in the stream, looking for newts. The time flew by, and when Dana realized how late it was, she hastily said good-bye to Kai and started for home.

She ran through the woods, crashing into bushes, tripping over roots, and brushing aside branches, indifferent to scratches and scrapes. When she came out into open country, the rim of the sun had just dipped below the horizon, streaking the clouds that had hidden it all day a greenish, fiery gold.

Dana raced across the meadow and jumped over the grange fence as the first few stars began to wink in the sky. She hadn't appeared for lunch or helped to pick tomatoes during the afternoon; dreading the reprimands that were sure to greet her, she slipped inside the house and paused to catch her breath. At the doorway to the dining room, she saw that her family had started supper without her. She took a few timid steps toward the table.

Her mother looked up, and Dana could tell that she had been crying.

"Good evening," she murmured, emboldened by the looks of relief on everyone's faces.

"Where were you?" asked one of her older brothers. "We were worried. We were going out to look for you after dinner."

She started to answer, but suddenly her mother was coming toward her, shoulders hunched and brows drawn together. Dana knew what was going to happen and took a step back.

The sound of the slap carried throughout the house.

Dana put her hand to her burning cheek and blinked back her tears. She knew that she deserved her mother's anger. She had seen with her own eyes what wolves did to lost calves, and when Dana hadn't shown up even for dinner, her family feared she had suffered the same fate.

"Where were you?" her mother cried. "Do you think it's all right to disappear like that, just for the fun of it?"

"I lost track of time," Dana mumbled. "I didn't realize how late it was. I'm sorry —"

A second slap stopped her words.

"I asked, where were you?"

"In the woods," said Dana, trembling, her voice barely audible.

"All day in the woods?" Her mother crossed her arms, disbelieving. "And may we know what you were doing there?"

"Exploring," Dana whispered. "Following a deer, eating wild blackberries . . . we even" — she caught her slip — "I even saw some bear cubs."

But her mother hadn't missed it. "We?" she asked. "Who was with you?"

Dana thought quickly. "Sara from the farm up north."

"Liar!" called out one of her sisters. "Sara was with *us*, picking tomatoes! We asked her about you, and she told us she hadn't seen you all day."

Her mother's hand shot forward and exploded against Dana's cheek. Dana moaned and huddled against the wall.

"Answer me! Who was with you?"

"Don't lie, Dana," said her father. "You are speaking to your mother. You made her suffer today. She thought something terrible had happened to you."

Dana scarcely heard him over her mother's screams. "Are you going to answer me?" She grabbed Dana's dress and shook her. "Answer me! *Who were you with?*"

Dana couldn't take anymore. "Kai," she shrieked. "I've been with Kai all day. Every day!"

"And who is this Kai?"

"I already . . . I told you once. He's my friend. My . . . my best friend. A boy my age."

Her mother released her. "Why are you lying to me?"

she asked, and this time her tone was not threatening but pained.

"I'm *not* lying!" Dana cried. "It's true. For a long time Kai has been coming to see me." She looked around the room. "Someone must have seen him. He's blond. . . ."

"She's crazy," said one of her younger brothers, but her mother silenced him with a glance.

"Kai doesn't exist," her oldest sister piped up. "She invented him. Haven't you noticed? She goes around talking to herself and muttering about Kai."

"I'm not lying!" Dana yelled, so furious that she no longer cared that she had worried them. "Kai exists. I see him every day! And I don't talk to myself!"

"You know there's no Kai, Dana," her older sister persisted. "He's just someone you've invented."

"No! He's real!" she howled. She turned and ran out of the house, letting the door slam behind her.

In the dining room, no one said anything. When they heard the door to the granary opening, Dana's mother sighed in relief. At least the girl had not run away.

She turned to her oldest daughter. "Next time, let me take care of her, all right?"

The girl gave her mother a sullen look, and silence again fell over the dining room.

In the granary, the only sounds were muffled sobs coming from the hayloft. Dana had taken refuge in her favorite corner, next to a small window; tonight it offered her a beautiful view of the darkening sky. She had often hidden here, away from the noise of her brothers and sisters, and she even kept a blanket nearby for warmth.

She wrapped herself in it now, because she planned to spend the night in the hayloft. She never wanted to live with her family again — they had turned into complete strangers. Her ears rang with her mother's yelling, the jeering of her brothers and sisters.

Liar! You're lying! Kai doesn't exist; you talk to yourself!

That was absurd. She didn't remember ever having talked to herself. But she couldn't think about it now, while her cheeks still burned from the slaps and her body still trembled from how hard her mother had shaken her.

She didn't hear Kai steal into the granary and softly close the door. He climbed up the ladder, pulled himself through the trapdoor, and went over to where she lay sobbing beneath the window.

"Dana, it's me," he whispered.

"Leave me alone!" The blanket muffled her voice and made her sound far away.

"Dana, I want to talk with you."

"Go away. You don't exist."

Kai shuddered as if he had received a blow.

"That's just what I want to talk to you about."

There was a brief silence, and then Dana's head of tangled hair emerged from beneath the blanket. Her skin was pale, her eyes red, and her nose puffy.

Kai sat down beside her. "I do exist. But no one else can see me. You're the only one."

Dana stared at him. "Are you teasing me?"

"You know I'm not. Think about it."

Dana closed her eyes. It didn't make sense, not when he knelt in front of her as real and worried as she was herself. But if Kai *weren't* telling the truth, how come her family had never seen him? And if they could see him, why would they say she talked to herself when he was right there?

"But why?" she asked, fear gripping her heart. "Why can't they see you? Who are you?"

"I'm your friend. That's the most important thing. And I will be your friend always, and I will always be with you. That's all there is to say."

"*All* there is to say? You think that explains everything — or *anything*?"

"What else can I say? You will have other friends that everyone can see. But many years from now, you'll realize you never had a better friend than me."

"How can you be so sure?" Dana blurted out, stunned by his conceit. She studied him a moment. "I'm not quite right in the head, am I?" she whispered. "I see things no one else can see."

"There's nothing wrong with your head." Kai smiled. "There's nothing bad in you at all. You're special, Dana, very special. That is why you can see me when no one else can."

"But maybe I don't want to be special," she said without thinking.

For a moment, Kai said nothing. Then he asked softly, "Do you want me to go away? Because if that's what you want, I'll leave. I will disappear from your life, and no one will ever cause you trouble again because of me."

Dana said nothing, just sat staring at him. She would miss him so much if he went away. Indeed, after the argument with her family, Kai was the only person who seemed near and real. She felt an impulse to hug him, but she held back; from the day she had tried to take his hand, she had not dared to try to touch him again. Now a sudden suspicion gripped her. Slowly she lifted her hand to pat her friend's cheek. He seemed to hesitate for a moment, but he didn't draw back.

Her hand went right through Kai's face as if he weren't there. She moved her hand back and forth in a desperate attempt to feel something, but although his body was perfectly opaque and visible, his image seemed as insubstantial as mist.

Dana moaned. She wished so desperately to be able to hold on to Kai, to keep him by her side, and now . . .

"I live on a different plane than you," he told her, his voice filled with sadness. "I wish it weren't so, but there's nothing I can do about it."

Dana moaned again. She did not know what Kai meant when he talked about "a different plane," but she did not want to ask him. She realized suddenly that she would rather not know, because it would suggest that the invisible barrier between them was higher even than she had imagined. . . . She pulled the blanket tighter around her and put her face to the window.

The stars glittered in the crisp, clear night. She felt something behind her and didn't have to turn to know that Kai was beside her. His arm slipped around her waist. The gentle pressure didn't feel like anything solid, more like the touch of the breeze, the warmth of a ray of sunlight. But it comforted her deeply in her loneliness, as Kai always had.

"Don't ever leave me, Kai," she whispered.

"Not ever," he promised.

2 The Man in the Gray Tunic

Two more years passed, and the friendship between Dana and Kai continued as strong as ever. The boy was cheerful and optimistic, and his company made Dana's life less monotonous. They couldn't keep track of all their adventures.

One afternoon when they were returning from the forest, talking and laughing as usual, Dana thought of their first meeting four years earlier. She recalled the skinny blond boy with the sincere eyes and friendly smile sitting on the rock wall near the barn. Now Kai was a good-looking boy of ten, though his smile was still sweet and friendly. More and more she had grown to trust him, and he hadn't yet disappointed her.

As she had promised, she never mentioned Kai to anyone. If her family happened to catch her talking to him, she pretended that he was nothing but a fancy of hers and she knew he didn't exist. She even laughed with her brothers and sisters when they teased her about her conversations with a friend no one could see. *He's real — they just don't understand,* she told herself. Even so, a small voice inside often whispered, "Are you sure you're not a little bit crazy?"

Dana knew that was what everyone thought. She let them think it. All she had to do was look in Kai's eyes and her doubts left her. She couldn't conceive of life without her best friend, and when she added things up, she realized that it was worth enduring her family's jeers if that was the price of having him around. Although she wanted to have a group of "normal" friends, she didn't want to lose the one friend who was most important to her.

Now, walking home beside Kai, Dana closed her eyes and let the breeze ruffle her long hair. Kai gazed at her fondly. Both of them were bathed in the magnificent light of the late autumn afternoon.

The breeze brought them voices from a distance. As they came to the edge of the meadow, Dana saw several girls her age tossing a rag doll back and forth. Sara, the daughter of the farmer to the north, seemed to be the leader.

Dana and Kai stopped several feet away, on the far side of the wall that marked the boundary between her family's and the neighbor's properties. Sara's team had the doll, and the other side was trying to take it away. The girls were yelling and jumping and laughing, their hair blowing and cheeks flushed. Dana wished that she could join them.

One of the girls noticed Dana standing by the wall and stopped to stare at her. The game came to a halt.

"What are *you* looking at?" the girl asked rudely.

A hard expression crossed Dana's face, and without answering, she turned to go.

"Wait," Sara called. "Do you want to play?"

The others grumbled, but Dana paid no attention to them. Was Sara teasing her? But the girl's face was friendly, and Dana decided to take a chance.

"I'd like to, very much," she replied.

Sara hesitated. "Well . . . actually," she said, "I'm not sure that would be a good idea. What if you threw the doll to someone who wasn't there?" She laughed loudly, and the others joined in.

"It would make more sense to throw it to one of you," Dana answered, smiling. "Otherwise, there wouldn't be any point to the game, would there?"

Sara seemed to appreciate Dana's graceful reply, but the others hooted louder than ever.

"Go talk with the devil, witch!" yelled one.

"That's right! Go talk with your own kind!" the others chorused.

Dana tried one more time. "I'm not a witch," she said. "I'm just like you. Except I like to think aloud, that's all."

"Then you think way too much!" another called out.

The girl who had the rag doll flung it hard at Dana's face. It hit her on the cheek and tumbled to the ground.

Dana bent to pick up the doll, dazed more from the girl's unbridled scorn than from the blow. Since she had the doll, maybe she could just join in the game by tossing it to Sara.

But Sara let the doll fly through her hands, and it fell to the grass.

Dana wasn't sure what to do. Before she could turn to leave, one of the girls picked up a rock and threw it at her. It hit Dana in the arm; it wasn't much bigger than a pebble, and it didn't really hurt. But that was all the others needed.

"Witch! Witch!" they called as they hurled their own stones. "Crazy witch!"

Dana covered her face with her hands and turned her back as the shower of stones came at her. She wanted to run, but pride made her walk away slowly, letting the rocks sting her body like needles. She wasn't sad. She didn't even feel like crying. All she felt was rage.

"Never again," she swore to Kai, who witnessed everything in silence. "Never again."

At the barn, they climbed up to the loft. Dana sat down by the small window and pulled her blanket around her.

"They say I'm a witch," she told Kai. "I wish I were. Then I could do terrible things to them and make them choke on all the awful things they said."

Kai knelt in front of her. "Don't ever say such a thing," he warned. "Don't even think it."

"Why not?"

"Because it's dangerous. You don't know what a wish can do. Besides, it isn't their fault."

"Oh no?" Dana jumped up. "And whose fault is it, then? Mine?"

Kai shook his head. "I don't know. Maybe it's mine. Maybe it's no one's."

Dana didn't answer. Right then it felt like her loneliness *was* Kai's fault.

"Try to understand them," he added. "They've been playing together since they were little, and you've never played with them. They barely know you. You're a stranger to them."

Dana watched Kai settle on the rough floorboards. She would never have been reasonable enough to think of that in her anger. *If you are my invention*, she said to herself, *how can you be so different from me?* In the time they'd spent together, Dana had come to know all of Kai's expressions and gestures: the tone of his voice; the gleam in his eyes; the way he pushed his blond hair back from his forehead; his athletic, confident movements. They weren't like hers, nor were they like anyone else's she knew. Furthermore, in their conversations he tended to put forth a point of view totally different from hers. Kai had to be more than her idea or image, more than just her imagination. And still she was the only one who believed he was real. . . .

She forced her mind back to the present. "Well . . . do you think that if I'd played with them before, they wouldn't have turned me away this time?"

"We live in a harsh land," Kai said. "People here struggle each day for survival. From the time they're children, they join together in groups; they feel safer that way."

"And they don't trust me because I haven't joined their group," Dana said in a low voice.

"Sooner or later you will find your place in the world," he reassured her. "Don't feel bad."

"Do you think I'm a witch, Kai?"

"I think you're Dana," he replied without a moment's hesitation. "And I don't care about anything else."

Dana moved closer to him, wanting more than anything to be able to nestle against something more substantial than air.

The winter arrived early, and it was an especially hard and cold one. The snow and ice ruined a large part of the harvest and killed many animals in the forests. Hungry wolves roamed down from the mountains in packs; necessity made them bold, and they attacked the farm animals, further reducing the resources of the grange families.

Things got no better with the coming of spring. The cold gave way to choking heat and the worst drought anyone in the district could remember. For a family of twelve, like Dana's, it was a time of catastrophe. Food was scarce; they all had to work harder than ever. Dana grew alarmingly thin, and so did everyone else. A mysterious sickness carried off one of her older sisters and a younger brother, as well as her grandfather.

Dana became even more silent, grimly so, working like a mule and never protesting; the activity helped to keep her from thinking. She spoke less with Kai, though he continued to assist her with her chores.

One morning she went to the well to draw water. It was a common well shared by several grange families, and because of the severity of the drought, water was now strictly rationed. Dana's family was allowed three buckets a day. She always had to make two trips because she could fit only two buckets on her barrow. Today when she lowered the first bucket to the bottom of the well, she heard only a small splash. Dana wondered whether there would be enough water to fill all three.

She pulled hard on the rope, and the full bucket slowly rose. As she lifted it, she saw Kai watching her closely.

"The water won't last much longer," she told him. She set the full bucket in the barrow, tied the second one to the rope, and lowered it into the well. They both heard it hit bottom, and Kai helped her pull it up.

Dana had often asked herself how it was possible for a

person whom she couldn't touch, who was as incorporeal as air or mist, to do things like gather eggs or pull a well rope. She had watched Kai many times to try to understand this, and the only thing she could see was that he appeared to have to concentrate very hard to accomplish the task. She knew it was pointless to ask him about it; he would never explain.

Dana set the bucket on the edge of the well and wiped the sweat from her brow with the back of her hand. A shadow fell across her face. She turned, and Kai too swung around abruptly.

A horseman had pulled up near them. His beautiful white horse was lathered with sweat and blowing from the heat.

"Beg pardon," he said pleasantly.

He was an old man with silver gray hair that cascaded to his shoulders like a waterfall. His deep-set, inquisitive eyes were also gray, as was the tunic he cinched with a leather belt. From it dangled an assortment of little pouches. He carried no weapons that Dana could see, and even though his white horse was magnificent, he seemed dressed too plainly to be a nobleman. Yet something set him above a simple country man.

"Forgive me for interrupting your work, girl," the horseman said, "but could you please tell me how to get to the city?"

Dana nodded down the lane. "You ride in that direction

as far as the next crossroad. Then you take the fork to the left, which will lead you there. It's only a day's ride from here."

"Crossroad, you say?" The horseman stood up in his stirrups to look down the hill.

"That way." Dana lifted her arm to point. The bucket sitting on the edge of the well teetered dangerously, and she hastened to steady it.

"Careful." He smiled, and a multitude of wrinkles formed around his mouth and eyes, making his weathered face seem older still. "You don't want to waste water in times like these."

Dana blushed and set the bucket in the barrow. The horseman watched for a moment, and then something behind her seemed to catch his eye. Suddenly his expression changed. His smile vanished and his gray eyes narrowed.

Dana turned to see what he was so intent upon — she had thought there was nothing behind her — and froze. There *was* nothing behind her . . . except Kai.

Quickly she turned back toward the old man. His face had recovered its pleasant expression.

"May God protect you, child," he told her. "And thank you. Don't worry about water. Tonight it will rain."

Dana stole a quick look at the sky — not a cloud in sight. She said nothing, however. Her mind was filled with the thought that Kai might have been seen by someone besides herself.

The man gave a slight nod, spurred his horse, and galloped off down the road. Dana stood where she was, her heart beating madly. The eddy of fine dust raised by his horse's hooves blazed golden in the sunlight.

When he was out of sight, Dana turned toward Kai. Before she could speak, he said forcefully, "He couldn't see me, it wasn't what you think. He wasn't even looking my way."

Despite the emphasis of his words, Dana saw a gleam of doubt in his eyes. She steadied her buckets and, with Kai's help, headed back to the house.

That afternoon Dana tried to bring up the subject of the horseman with Kai. She remembered perfectly the man's expression as he had gazed behind her, his mixture of amazement and curiosity; she also remembered that Kai seemed as surprised by the man's perception as she was. If the old man had seen Kai . . . that proved that she wasn't crazy, that her friend really did exist, and people would believe her at last.

But Kai didn't seem eager to recall the scene at the well, at first trying to change the subject. When she persisted, he cut her short: The old man hadn't seen him; it was all her imagination. "Just forget it," he said.

"But why?" Dana asked.

"Because there was something strange about him that is better not to dwell on," Kai answered. "Besides, it's almost certain we won't see him again."

Dana decided to drop the question. She knew she wouldn't get any further with Kai, at least not then.

But she had reason to remember the horseman in the gray tunic much sooner than she expected.

That night, exactly as he had predicted, it rained.

3
The Tower

The hard rain improved conditions for a little while, but the damage from the drought was irreparable. The crops baked in the fields, fires ravaged the forests, and many of the grange animals died from the heat or had to be sacrificed to the family's survival. The whole region suffered. Dana was thankful for Kai's unconditional support, but she could not help wondering when things would change.

One afternoon as she and Kai returned from the fields, she noticed that only her younger brothers and sisters were outside — she didn't see an adult anywhere. Odder still, the door to the house, which was always kept open because of the heat, stood firmly shut.

They went to the stable seeking shade and were surprised by what they found there. The drought had left Dana's family with only two cows and a draft horse. But now there were two new mounts in the shed: a white horse and a young bay mare. Kai whistled admiringly at the two superb animals.

"They can't be ours! We don't have any money," Dana said. She looked at Kai.

"Visitors," he murmured.

She glanced at the white horse, wondering why it looked familiar. Her siblings on the porch had little to say. The most she could guess was that the adults of her family were meeting with the visitors. Dana knew the side window would be open to catch any breeze. If she crouched beneath it, perhaps she could listen without being seen.

She could hear her parents' voices clearly, and occasionally that of an older brother, as well as the voice of a stranger, a man, to whom the horses must belong.

"I can assure you that I will take very good care of her," the stranger was saying. "I will provide food, clothing, the security of a home, and an education that would never be available to her here."

Dana frowned. She had heard that voice before: calm, low, pleasant.

"We realize that this is a fine opportunity," her father replied. "But these are hard times, and a farm family cannot give up a pair of arms that do good work."

"But it would also be one less mouth to feed," the man answered. "And I will be happy to compensate you for any loss."

"Money cannot take the place of a daughter," Dana's mother objected, her tone harsh.

They must be negotiating the marriage of one of Dana's older sisters. Dana turned toward Kai to tell him it was nothing serious, but the words froze on her tongue at the worried expression on his face.

"I admit that I would be taking her far away," the stranger was saying, "but I am offering her something that is within the reach of very few. Such an opportunity should not be wasted in times like these."

At that instant Dana felt her heart stop; she had heard almost those very words in that same voice beside the well a few weeks ago, when an old man in a gray tunic had asked her the way to the city.

She looked at Kai, but he seemed somewhere far away.

"If Dana comes with me, she will never be hungry," the stranger pressed.

What? They were talking about *her*?!? Dana felt faint and clung to the wall. Her parents were talking about marrying her to the man in the gray tunic! She knew it was common for the parents of a young girl to negotiate the matter of her marriage with her suitors, but she was only ten years old! She had never imagined that such a thing could happen to her, especially with an old man she didn't know, no matter how wealthy he might be.

Distraught, she tried to attract Kai's attention, and this time his green eyes looked into hers.

"It will all work out," he murmured, but his voice wavered.

She heard her father saying, "Very well, you may take her. Will you be leaving tonight?"

"No!" Dana shouted. She pushed away from the window, her head spinning.

She knew the people in the dining room must have heard her, but she couldn't face them. She ran to the granary, and within minutes she was trembling beneath her blanket, fully aware that they would soon come looking for her.

She felt Kai beside her, and that comforted her. If he was there, nothing could be so very terrible. Then she remembered that her future husband might know of Kai's existence, and that made her even more afraid. The man would never let them stay together, never. . . .

"Run away," said Kai.

Dana was about to answer that she had been thinking the same thing when she realized that Kai hadn't said, "Let's run away" — he had referred only to her.

"Would you come with me?" she asked.

"Away from the grange?" He shook his head. "I can't."

"Why not?" she demanded, but just then she heard the granary door open.

"Too late," Kai murmured.

Dana shrank into her corner. There was no way out now. As she listened to someone climbing the wood ladder, she clung to the idea that at least with the money the stranger had promised, her brothers and sisters would be able to eat.

"Dana?" It was her mother. "Dana, child, you're here."

Dana pulled the blanket tighter around her, despite the heat, and looked at her mother warily.

"It's for your own good," said her mother. "You will never be hungry with this gentleman, or work yourself to an early death. Besides, he will give you an education that we can't provide. You will be something more in life than a simple farm girl."

"And he will give you a lot of money for me," Dana added bitterly.

Her mother looked hurt. "You think we're selling you, is that it? Many families would happily *pay* to give their daughters this opportunity. Your brothers and sisters are envious of your good fortune, Dana. They will never see anything beyond this grange, this village, maybe this district. You've been given a gift from heaven."

Dana hesitated. Her mother came nearer, and suddenly Dana was in her arms.

"Oh, my little girl," said her mother. "You're still very young to be leaving your home . . . but if we let this opportunity pass, it may never come again."

"I don't want to leave, Mother," Dana confessed. "I don't like that man."

"He won't harm you, my sweet child. But listen. If the day comes that you cannot bear your new life, and you find that you are not happy, you don't have to stay there. If you come back home, we will welcome you with open arms."

Dana's mother took something from her pocket and put it in her daughter's hand. Dana studied it with curiosity. It was a strange metal amulet in the shape of a crescent moon, and between the two points was a six-pointed star.

"This belonged to my mother, and to my mother's mother, and to her mother as well. It will protect you from all harm, and it will remind you that here on the grange, I will always be thinking of you. Take good care of it."

Dana was moved by this show of affection; her mother was not often given to such displays. She hung the talisman around her neck and hugged her mother in thanks.

The good-byes, packing her few belongings. . . . All that took only the afternoon, and it happened as if in a dream. But when Dana met the penetrating eyes of the visitor, she came totally awake.

"Are you ready, child?" he asked pleasantly.

"Yes," said Dana, shifting from one foot to the other. She had only a vague idea of what marriage was and what was involved, and although she was surprised that they were not going to perform the wedding ceremony in the presence of her family, the excitement of the coming journey wiped those thoughts from her mind.

She followed the man in the gray tunic into the stable,

where he pointed at the magnificent bay mare. "She's yours. Go to her, talk to her, get to know her."

Dana had been around only slow-witted farm horses before, never a high-spirited, powerful horse like this one, bred exclusively to be ridden. She approached the mare hesitantly, but soon she was stroking the silky hide, whispering soft words into the bay's ear.

"She likes me."

The man smiled. "You must give her a name; that way she will be completely yours."

Dana did not have to think long. "Moonstar," she said, touching the charm her mother had given her.

They led their horses out of the stable to the yard in front of the house. Dana's family had lined up to say good-bye, and she shivered as she realized this might be the last time she'd see them all.

"Don't be afraid," her companion said softly. "Are you ready?"

Dana was about to say yes, but she felt as if something were missing. Her eyes traveled across the grange and her assembled family. *Kai!* she thought. Why wasn't he here with her? She couldn't leave without him!

"Just one minute, please," she told the visitor.

She ran to the granary door and peered inside. "Kai?" she called in a low voice.

There was no answer. She looked all over the granary, growing more and more alarmed. What would she do if he didn't want to come with her?

"Kai!" she yelled, not caring if her family heard her.

"I'm here, Dana." His voice came from close behind her.

She turned and nearly wept with relief. He walked out from behind the ladder to the hayloft, his steps reluctant and slow.

"You're leaving," he said sadly.

"*We're* leaving," she corrected him. "I want you to come with me."

"But I can't—"

"I won't go anywhere without you," she interrupted him, shaking her black curls vigorously.

The sadness in his face seemed to deepen further. "Really, I want to . . ." Kai began, but he stopped as they heard the squeak of the granary door. The man in the gray tunic appeared in the entrance.

"Is something the matter?" he asked.

Dana twisted her hands, staring at the floor. "It's just that I can't . . ." she began.

A gleam of understanding appeared in the stranger's gray eyes. He looked toward the spot where Kai stood—this time there could be no doubt—and said, "You can come too." He made a brief pass with his hand, lightly tracing a circle in the air. And Dana had a strange sensation, as if something invisible had broken.

Kai's face suddenly shone with joy. "Tell him thanks," he said to Dana, and when she said nothing for a moment, he thumped her with his elbow.

"Thank you!" she blurted out, almost without realizing it.

So now it was time to say good-bye to the grange and her family, time to follow the horseman in the gray tunic and to try to keep her seat, with Kai behind her, on her new bay mare. Along the road they came upon Sara and her sister on their way back from town. Dana sat up as straight as she could on Moonstar and was pleased to see the openmouthed look of disbelief and envy on her neighbor's face.

It made her feel a little better.

Soon it was sundown, but they rode much of the night, always toward the east, until they reached the third town from the grange. There they stopped at an inn.

Dana had not yet dared to ask her companion anything. She had her own room at the inn, but she was too tired to appreciate it, and too confused to try to learn anything more about her fate. She fell straight to sleep, Kai close beside her.

The next day they got under way shortly after sunrise. When her mind was a little clearer, Dana realized that she did not even know her guide's name, and with many stammers and blushes, she asked him.

"You can call me Maestro," he said, "since I will be your teacher."

That seemed to her a strange name to call the man who was going to be her husband, but she made no objection.

When the Maestro saw that Dana had gained better control of Moonstar, he spurred Midnight, his white horse, to a trot. Dana's mare immediately followed. Dana held on tight and tried to adjust to the new gait. Given confidence by Kai's crystalline laughter behind her, she sat up proudly in her saddle and settled easily into the faster speed. Later they even moved into a canter, which she found very pleasant. Riding Moonstar so steadily with Kai close behind her, she felt that even the sun wasn't so burning hot.

Several days more went by. To Dana it seemed an eternity, because her guide seldom spoke, and she didn't allow herself to talk with Kai in front of other people. The sun shone down pitilessly, and they rested only when absolutely necessary.

In the third week, the road ahead seemed to disappear into an enormous chain of mountains that stood before them like a row of sharp, menacing teeth. The highest peaks were covered with snow, while the slopes wore a dense woodsy mantle.

The Maestro broke his usual silence to say, "The Tower stands in the Valley of the Wolves, in that mountain range."

"The Tower?" Dana asked. "Is that the place we're going?"

The Maestro nodded. "That is my home."

"A little isolated in those mountains," Kai whispered in Dana's ear.

She'd had the same thought. She didn't ask any more questions, but she was fascinated. In every town they had stopped, the villagers had treated the Maestro with respect if not something like fear. It was obvious that the man had money, but Dana began to sense that there was more to it than that, something she hadn't yet comprehended.

That night they stayed at another inn near the side of the road. Dana sat by a window in the darkness of her room. "There are so many things I want to know! Why did the Maestro choose me out of all my sisters? How can he see you, Kai?"

"He can't see me," Kai murmured in a sleepy voice.

Dana turned from the window. "You must really think I'm stupid," she snapped. "What are you hiding from me?"

Kai sat up, his hair every which way. "I have a few answers," he said. "Or at least I think I do. But I have even more questions. I can't tell you anything for sure yet."

"But he sees you, doesn't he? I saw him speak to you!"

Kai scratched his head. "I don't think he does. I've tested it, and it seems to me that he only knows I'm there, that he knows roughly where I am every minute. But he can't see me or hear me the way you can."

"How strange! What else have you found out?"

"Nothing else."

Dana blew out her breath and turned back to her reflection in the window. "You're lying."

"Dana, don't be angry with me." Kai moved over to

whisper in her ear. "I'm sure we will understand everything when we reach the Tower."

Dana shuddered when she heard that word.

"Are you afraid?" he asked.

She nodded and rested her elbows on the windowsill. Kai's shoulder leaned against hers. As usual, it wasn't an ordinary physical contact, but that didn't matter to Dana. In fact, over time she'd grown so accustomed to that gentle sensation that it felt strange to touch anyone else.

"What matters is that we're together," he said.

Dana pressed Kai's hand, closing her fingers over empty space.

Three days later they reached the foothills of the mountains and rode through a narrow pass. The air here was purer and cooler, and Dana was grateful for the change, although the great blocks of gray rock that rose above the trail intimidated her. Midnight seemed to know the path, however, and moved forward confidently. Moonstar followed.

That night, and the next two, they slept out in the open. Dana curled up in her old blanket while the Maestro sat near the fire contemplating the flames, his face like stone. The night wind roaring against the rocks of the cordillera brought the distant howling of wolves, and his presence by the fire reassured her. She still had many questions about him, but remained too nervous to speak to him often.

On the fourth evening, they came to a spot where the pass opened onto a small valley enclosed by mountains. Down to her left, Dana could make out the houses of a tiny town. On the far side of the valley, the mountains were covered by a thickly wooded forest wrapped in shreds of mist.

"Welcome to the Valley of the Wolves," said the Maestro.

"Where is the Tower?" Dana asked, stretching her neck to see better. "In the town?"

The Maestro shook his head and pointed to a dot barely visible through the mist. "There, at the edge of the woods."

"That really *is* isolated," Kai remarked.

They spent the night in the town. Dana did not miss the fact that her companion was no stranger there, but she also saw how the townspeople seemed uneasy in his presence and drew back at his approach.

"Have you noticed, Kai?" she asked him when they were alone in her room at the inn. "The people in this town don't seem to trust the Maestro. I wonder why?"

Kai shrugged. "Maybe they think he's strange, living in a tower," he said. "But if my suspicions are right, I'm not surprised that people are wary of him."

Dana gave Kai an inquisitive look, but he put a finger to his lips. From the gleam in his eyes, she knew that he was not going to tell her anything more just now, so she pretended to be cross and tossed a pillow at his head.

It passed right through Kai and smacked against the wall.

The Maestro woke Dana later than usual, when the sun was already high in the sky. He didn't offer an explanation, but she supposed he had let her rest in order to gain back some strength — a much-needed break after the long, tiring trip.

They passed through the Valley of the Wolves without incident, and when the shadows of the forest were closing in on them, they came to a turn. There, outlined against the mountains and rising above the trees, was the slim silhouette of a tower. Tall and elegant, it was crowned by a long needlelike spire. A small crenellated balcony ringed the Tower near its top.

Dana liked it, despite the eerie feeling it gave her.

"Beautiful, isn't it?" said the Maestro. "It was built to act as a link between the celestial levels and the earthly planes. The needle collects the forces of the firmament, and the foundations are deeply sunk into Mother Earth. The Tower joins beauty and power."

Dana nodded, though this explanation made no sense to her. "It looks like a giant came and drove it into the ground and then went away," she commented, and immediately felt that she'd said something stupid.

But the Maestro did not seem to be listening. He touched his spurs to Midnight and they went on their way, following a narrow trail through the forest. Soon they lost sight of the Tower. The fog grew thicker and the wind whistled among the tree branches. As the sun dropped low in the sky, wolves started to howl in the mountains. Dana became uneasy.

"Don't be afraid, child," the Maestro said. "The wolves can't harm us yet, not until nightfall."

Dana leaned back in her saddle to take comfort from Kai, who slipped his arms around her waist. She gave him a quick smile over her shoulder.

Just as the sun sank below the horizon, they emerged from the forest. At the far side of a large field, encircled by a black fence, the Tower rose in all its grandeur. It was much taller than Dana had thought.

"My home," the Maestro murmured.

"Look." Kai pointed to the top.

Dana looked up and saw, in the pale twilight, a figure standing between the merlons of the balcony. A long billowing cape swirled in the wind. Dana thought it was probably someone posted as a lookout, but she was too far away to tell whether it was a man or a woman.

"We're expected," said the Maestro, smiling, when he noticed where Dana was looking.

Again he spurred his horse, and Midnight set off at a gallop toward the Tower. Not to be outdone, Moonstar followed.

Dana screamed and held on tight to the reins: She had never galloped before, but she liked the sensation nevertheless. It was like flying, with the wind blasting her face and her black mane streaming behind her, and feeling the elegant movement of the bay mare's muscles pulsing against her calves.

When Moonstar stopped beside Midnight at the black iron fence, Dana settled herself in the saddle and watched as the Maestro, sitting straight-backed with one arm outstretched, uttered a few unintelligible words in the direction of the gate. She saw a spark burst from his fingertips. Then, with a creaking noise, the gate swung open.

She gulped in surprise. Though it was growing darker by the minute, she was pretty sure that no one had come to open the gate.

The Maestro turned toward her. "Please, enter."

Dana lightly kicked her horse, and Moonstar passed through with no hesitation at all.

A narrow path cut through a dark, labyrinthine garden directly to the Tower. Dana looked up, but the figure between the merlons had disappeared.

"Welcome to the Tower," the Maestro said from behind her. "One of the few academies of high sorcery left in the world today. You may consider yourself extremely fortunate to have been admitted as an apprentice. Many would kill for such an honor."

"That's what I suspected," Kai murmured.

High sorcery . . . apprentice . . . the Tower . . .

Then I haven't been brought here to marry the Maestro? Dana thought to herself, almost swooning. What about the conversation she'd overheard at the grange? When she recalled it, she realized that her parents and the visitor must not have been talking about marriage but about schooling of some sort. Flooded with relief, she squeezed the talisman her mother had given her.

"Come along," the Maestro urged.

As she rode toward the Tower, Dana tried to take in this surprising change of fortune. She wasn't going to be married. She was going to be trained in sorcery, just as in Kai's stories. The Maestro had apparently sought her out for that purpose. He must think she was special — perhaps it had something to do with the way she could see Kai. It suddenly occurred to her that here she might be able to find out more about Kai, perhaps even discover a way to make him a person like everyone else.

Almost at the same time came the echo of a memory that now seemed very far away: the girls yelling, "Go talk with your own kind, witch!"

Dana could not hide a broad smile. "Yes, I am a witch," she told herself. "Or at least I soon will be."

They stopped in front of a great oak door and dismounted from their horses, which trotted obediently off to the stables. The Maestro repeated the opening spell, and as the door swung wide, Dana clasped Kai's hand, delighted with this new turn of events. Kai must have felt as excited as she was, because the contact seemed almost real.

4 First Lessons

No cock crowed at the break of dawn, but Dana was used to getting up without anyone having to call her. She came awake with the odd sense of not knowing where she was. Then the events of yesterday evening flashed before her, and she hurried to the window to see the view from her new home.

The outlook from the Tower was magnificent. The sun was beginning to peep from behind the mountains, burning off the ghostly mists that enveloped the woods. In the distance, the town stirred beneath the first glow of dawn.

She turned around to look at her room and felt satisfied. Though the chamber was not very large and only sparsely furnished, it was nevertheless more than she had known at the grange. Someone had placed a tray with a delicious-looking breakfast on the table before her, and several pieces of clothing had been carefully laid over the back of a chair. She went over to inspect them and found two white tunics, a warm gray cape, and a leather belt.

"My new uniform!" she exclaimed. She wanted to show Kai, but he didn't seem to be around. She supposed that he had gone out to explore the Tower on his own.

She decided to change her worn clothing for one of the tunics, and discovered that it fit as if it had been made for her. Since it wasn't cold, she left the cape on the chair. Then she hurried over to eat her breakfast.

As she ate, she asked herself how someone could have stolen into her room without her being aware of it. She always slept very lightly, but last night, her first night in the Tower, she obviously hadn't stirred. Whoever it was must have been as stealthy as a cat.

Dana shook her head. She supposed that in an academy of high sorcery, things often happened that had no ordinary explanations, and she would quickly grow used to it.

She made her bed, washed her hands and face in the basin, and then wondered what to do next. Should she wait for someone to come? Or should she go looking for the Maestro? What if she left her room and he didn't like it that she was nosing around the Tower? She waited on the edge of the bed for a while, but since no one came to collect her, she decided that she wasn't going to sit around all day doing nothing. She went to the door and looked out into the corridor.

No one appeared, and no sound broke the heavy silence. Dana stepped outside, closing the door softly, and started down the hall, with no idea at all where she was going or what she was looking for.

She soon found that the Tower was a labyrinth of rooms, stairways, and corridors. In some rooms the walls were so bare she could see the cold gray stone, while others were lined with warm, rich tapestries and carpets. Some were furnished in an orderly, elegant style; some were empty. And still others seemed to serve as huge storerooms in which strange dust-covered objects of every imaginable shape, color, and size were piled on top of one another. In many rooms the beds were made up, though she didn't see a soul anywhere who might be using them.

After a while she came across an enormous spiral stairway that she guessed was at the center of the Tower. It seemed to serve as the Tower's spine, running from the ground to the very top. Dana pictured the arrangement of rooms, a plan repeated on each floor. The layout was not as confusing as it first seemed.

But what concerned her most was that she didn't see another soul anywhere. Weren't there other students besides herself? If so, where were they? And where was Kai?

On the stairway the night before, she had passed someone tall swathed in a cape. A hood had hidden the person's face. Though she'd only had a glance, something odd had struck her. What was it? She couldn't remember. She'd been too sleepy to pay much attention.

She wandered though more rooms and climbed up and down more stairs, amazed at how enormous the Tower was and how empty it seemed to be. She came upon a large, closed door with a placard on it. Since she didn't know how to read, Dana ignored the sign, but from the size of the door and the complicated, curlicue designs on it, she thought it must lead to something important.

She tried the doorknob, suspecting it would be locked — she guessed magicians guarded their secrets well. To her surprise, however, the door opened smoothly, and Dana slipped inside.

She found herself in a huge room that seemed to occupy almost half a floor of the Tower. It was filled with tall shelves containing books, parchments, and papers piled up in cheerful disarray. She began to explore and was soon lost in a maze of bookshelves.

She had never imagined so many books in one place. *They must reveal so many interesting things*, she thought wistfully. She had always believed that it would be wonderful to read, although like most of the country people in her region, her family had no opportunity to learn the written word.

She went up and down the aisles until she discovered a central space occupied by a very large oval walnut table and several chairs. She circled the table, saw nothing especially interesting on it, and started down another book-lined aisle.

She turned a corner . . . and almost tripped over someone sitting on the floor. "Sorry!" she exclaimed, suddenly frightened as she imagined what an angry magician might do to her.

But the reader didn't look up from his book, only murmured something in a language Dana couldn't understand. It didn't sound harsh — she didn't think it was a curse — but it gave her the feeling that the person was annoyed at being disturbed.

Dana was wondering whether to run away or apologize again when the individual stood up to a full six feet and stared down at her. She froze in pure astonishment.

Before her was a creature of a wild and childish beauty, of delicate features and enormous topaz eyes, like those of a cat. Fine, copper-colored hair spilled over his long and pointed ears, and a violet tunic covered his slender, fine-boned body.

Dana realized that she was staring and lowered her eyes, feeling her cheeks flame.

This strange being tilted his head to one side and examined her with curiosity. "You've never seen an elf before, have you?" he asked softly. He had a pleasant, musical manner of speaking, although the tone of his voice was rather cool and distant.

"No," Dana said in a low voice. "I'm sorry."

"Don't be sorry," the elf said. "There's a first time for everything." He turned his attention back to the parchment he was reading, and his long, fine fingers danced across the words. "Were you looking for something special?"

"I was looking for some*one*. Anyone. I'm lost, I think. I arrived last night."

"I know. I saw you on the stairs, but you may not remember."

"Only a little."

The elf did not answer, and Dana felt she should leave. But where would she go?

"Where is the Maestro?" she asked.

The elf's lips lifted in a slight smile, but he did not take his strange golden eyes from his manuscript. "In his chambers. In the highest part of the Tower, above the balcony with the merlons."

As Dana turned to leave, the elf added, "I tell you that so you will know that you are never to go there. Take my advice. He doesn't like anyone to enter his domain without an invitation. Not even I can do that."

Dana looked at him quizzically. "Are you an apprentice like me?"

Now the elf did look up, and his eyes bore into hers. "I am an apprentice, but not like you. I have been studying many years. I finished the Book of Water some time ago. You, on the other hand, have just arrived, as you said yourself."

Again Dana felt herself blush. "I'm . . . I'm very sorry," she stammered. "I . . ."

"Doesn't matter." He turned back to his parchment.

"What do I do? Where are the others?"

"What others?"

"The other apprentices."

Once again a faint smile crossed his lips. "We're the only ones. This is a very select school."

"But all those rooms! Are they really empty?"

"These are bad times for magic," was his answer.

Dana wasn't sure what he meant. The elf looked at her again, this time with a spark of friendliness in his eyes. "My name is Fenris. Well, to tell the truth, it isn't, really, but my elfin name is very difficult to pronounce. So just call me Fenris. It's a kind of abbreviation."

"I'm happy to. I'm Dana."

The elf nodded and went back to reading. "The Maestro will call you when he wants to give you your first lesson," he said.

"You and I won't be together then?"

Fenris shook his head. "You need to begin at the beginning. I'm much further along. But don't worry, you humans learn very quickly."

Dana could think of nothing more to say, so she said good-bye and left the library.

When she got back to her room, Kai was sitting on her bed. He had also been exploring the Tower, and the two friends told each other their discoveries.

"Did you go up to the top?" Dana asked.

"I didn't dare go past the balcony," Kai answered.

"There's a lot of power focused there, and I didn't like the way it made me feel. Whoever controls those rooms must control the entire Tower."

"Fenris told me it's where the Maestro lives."

Kai nodded. "Then it's as I thought — he is a very powerful man."

Dana and Kai stayed in her room the rest of the morning. By noon she was so hungry that she had almost decided to search out the elf, when suddenly the door to her room opened and a full tray of food came in. A little cry escaped Dana's lips — no one seemed to be holding the tray. With a closer look, however, she realized that someone very short was carrying it. The person's head was hidden behind the water pitcher, but Dana could hear panting and puffing.

"Here you are!" a snippet of a woman exclaimed, heaving the tray onto the table with none too much delicacy. "Every day it gets harder for me to climb those blessed stairs. One of these days they're going to do me in!"

Dana blinked and looked again. Before her stood a tiny, round, robust woman not much more than three feet tall. When she walked she rocked from side to side, and her hard-soled boots slapped on the stone floor.

"Don't stare at her like that, it's not polite," whispered Kai.

Dana had heard about dwarves in the stories Kai told her. The legends said that far to the north, there rose a great mountain chain whose peaks reached the sky, and deep in their bowels, dwarves lived in tunnels they had hollowed from the rock. They were a small people, but strong and fierce, and very skillful in forging weapons and tools from the metals they mined in the mountains.

What a dwarf was doing so far south, Dana didn't know; but neither could she imagine what an elf could be doing so far from the magical elfin lands that, it was said, stretched beyond the sea. The dwarf was so different from the elf she'd just met that she wondered if all of this weren't simply a dream.

"I've brought your food up here *twice* today!" the dwarf said, pointing a fat finger at Dana. "But this is the last time. Don't think that just because you're a fine little miss you have more rights than anyone else. We women work as hard as the men, here like everywhere else! You hear what I say?"

"Oh, yes, ma'am," Dana replied quickly.

"Well, you seem to have a few manners. Where do you come from?"

"From the grange. My name's Dana."

The dwarf harrumphed and shook her head. "So now we have a little farmer girl. What is that old goat up to?"

Did she mean the Maestro? Dana was awed at the woman's daring.

"All right now, you listen," the dwarf said. "My name is Maritta. If you ever need me for anything that isn't spouting off some rigmarole or conjuring up thunder and lightning, look for me on the very bottom floor, in the kitchen. All right?"

Dana nodded.

Maritta, hands on her hips and frowning, looked her up and down. Finally she seemed satisfied and turned to leave.

"Oh, yes," she said from the door, "when you get hungry, *you* come down. You're young. Don't make me come up here. I'm not eighty anymore!"

Dana promised she would come down, and the dwarf left, letting the door bang behind her. Dana and Kai heard her groan her way down the stairs.

"She's a lively one," Dana remarked. "With all the noise she makes, I can't imagine why I didn't hear her this morning when she brought in my tray."

She ate a leisurely lunch and then ventured down to the kitchen with the empty tray. Now that she understood the structure of the Tower a little better, it proved easy to find. Maritta's territory occupied a large, generous space on the ground floor that opened onto a back terrace. The dwarf stood on a stool, working at the sink.

"I brought this down for you," Dana told her.

Maritta pointed to a table and went back to scrubbing the sink.

Dana looked around. In that whole huge kitchen, there was no one but the dwarf. "Do you really work here all by yourself?" she asked.

"I don't have all that much work," Maritta answered.

"Up to now I've only had to feed two crazy magicians and two horses. Now it's three and three. So what? I don't need anyone else down here; they'd just get in the way. Besides, the Maestro is an old man and eats like a bird, and that elf is so thin, he fills up fast. I'm hoping that you have a good appetite, miss, or my talents as a cook are never going to see the light!"

Dana laughed. "And who brings the food from town?" she asked.

"From town?" Maritta shrugged. "Child, this is the Tower. The pantry is never empty here. You'll get used to it. Even I have, and that wasn't easy; we dwarves have little faith in magic."

When Dana went back to her room, she found a new surprise. Kai was no longer in the room, but the Maestro, the Lord of the Tower, was standing by the window, waiting for her.

"Good afternoon, Dana."

"Good afternoon," she replied.

The magus pointed to a chair and Dana sat down. She noticed that there was a book on the table. She couldn't read the gold letters on the cover, but she made out the image of a tree tooled in the leather beneath them.

The Lord of the Tower walked back and forth for a while. "The study of magic is a very long process," he finally began. "You should know that there are five levels. The white tunic you're wearing symbolizes the very first level, that of a student who as yet knows nothing. Do you know what that is I've left you on the table?"

"A book," said Dana.

"It is a book," the Maestro said, "but not just any book. It is the Book of Earth. In it you will learn the most fundamental level of magic, the one that teaches the sorcerer to decipher the language of the world. When you have mastered all the exercises in this volume, you will be able to do many things, from making a seed sprout in the palm of your hand to provoking an earthquake. Then there will be an examination, and, if you pass, you will exchange your white tunic for a green one, which will indicate that you are a second-level apprentice. Then you will progress through the Books of Air, Water, and finally Fire. But before anything else, you must learn one thing. Can you guess what it is?"

"Learn to read?" Dana ventured.

The Maestro frowned. "That goes without saying. But you needn't worry, you will master that quickly. You must also learn the language of the arcane, the language of magic, in which all spells are written. But that is not what I was referring to. No, this one thing is entirely different." He stopped pacing to look at her. "You must open your senses to magic."

Dana started to ask what he meant, but the Lord of the Tower came over to her and placed a bony hand on her shoulder. And suddenly everything began to spin.

Dana screamed and closed her eyes. She felt as if her breath were being sucked out by a powerful whirlwind. When the dizziness became unbearable, everything stopped as suddenly as it had begun.

Dana slowly opened her eyes and looked around.

She was no longer sitting in her room in the Tower but outdoors on the grass, in the middle of a circle of trees. At first she thought that time had run backward and that she was in the woods near the grange, or that everything had been a dream and the man in the gray tunic had never crossed her path.

Then she saw the Maestro standing beside her, smiling.

"You will become accustomed to teletransportation," he said, as Dana was still very pale. "We are in the woods surrounding the Tower."

"What are we doing here?"

The magician gestured with a sweep of his arm. "Listen carefully," he said. "The world functions according to a complex equilibrium. All living creatures struggle for survival — to grow taller, stronger, larger than any other, to dominate more territory, to have more descendants, to live more years. All of that requires energy. And energy, which might also be called magic, circulates through the world in endless cycles, never stopping. Energy is the soul of the earth, and all creatures are involved in its rhythms.

"Consider a rabbit. It eats grass, which provides

the energy for its survival. This is the same energy that the grass drew from the earth, the same energy that the wolf will obtain when it eats the rabbit. Do you understand?"

Dana nodded — she thought she at least grasped the main idea. From the corner of her eye she saw Kai stroll into the clearing and settle down against a nearby tree.

"Life is a constant battle to channel the world's energy, and getting one's own share of it means depriving other creatures of theirs. Look over there."

The Maestro pointed in front of him. At first Dana saw nothing but the trunk of an enormous tree. She followed it upward until she had to tip her head back to see the top of the gigantic organism.

"The king of the forest," the Maestro murmured, "but at what cost?"

Dana could see what he meant. No other trees grew around the giant, and many had died because its enormous branches blocked out the rays of the sun.

"But for every situation," the Maestro continued, pointing to the tree's foot, "there is always some form of life to take advantage of it."

And indeed, many ferns were growing at the base of the giant, enjoying the moisture and shade there. "Perhaps someday these plants will choke out the tree's roots and cause it to fall," the magician said quietly. "That's how it is. That is how the world functions."

Dana nodded, although she wasn't sure what the Maestro meant by all this.

"Life is the one goal of every creature. And every creature will do anything it can to prolong its life and the lives of its children. Once you understand that, you will understand the world, and it will be easier for you to control it."

He started off through the trees. Dana followed, and Kai after her.

"Magic is as simple as that — comprehending and controlling the energy that moves the world. Sorcerers know at every moment how that energy is flowing and use it to their advantage in order to change the world as they will. The more their wishes go against natural laws, the more energy they will need."

He stopped abruptly. "And now, my dear pupil, the moment has come to see how well you have assimilated my teaching." He pointed to a small sapling growing somewhat apart. "Tell me, what is that tree feeling?"

"Feeling?" Dana turned to him, confused, but his gray eyes were severe, forbidding her to say more.

At a loss, she walked over to the tree. It seemed to be an ordinary sapling. What could he want? She glanced at the Maestro for help, but his stony expression sent her back to the tree with full concentration. As she stood there examining it, she noticed that its leaves had lost their greenness and that its branches looked a little droopy.

What was the matter with it? She knew nothing about taking care of trees. Dana tossed her head. What did the Maestro expect of her? She struggled to review what he had told her about the world's energy.

Life is the one goal of every creature. . . . Once you understand that, you will understand the world, and it will be easier for you to control it.

Again Dana looked at the small tree. *Once you understand that . . .*

"This tree is sick," she announced.

The Maestro nodded. "And why?"

"How can I know that?"

"Listen to what it has to tell you. Open your senses."

"He wants you to feel the flow of the tree's energy," Kai said.

"And how do I do that?"

She realized she'd spoken loudly enough for the magician to hear her, and she eyed him nervously. The Lord of the Tower, however, had not moved.

To feel the flow of the energy . . .

Well, she didn't want to simply stand there like a ninny. She placed her hand on the rough bark of the tree and stroked it as if it were the silky coat of a cat.

Open your senses.

"Tell me what is hurting you," she said to the tree.

"You can do it," the Maestro told her, "or else I wouldn't have asked you to try."

His words made Dana feel a little less ridiculous. She closed her eyes to try to sense something, however slight it might be.

"Tell me. . . ."

With that, she felt a faint shiver on her fingertips, a

small flash of pain, so brief and weak that for a moment she thought she had imagined it. Gingerly, she placed her other hand on the bark and felt along the trunk.

Nothing happened. Dana stepped back from the tree.

"Don't worry," the magician told her. "Take your time. Gradually your sensitivity will become more refined, and you will be able to perceive sensations like the ones you first felt — and many more. All that will, of course, require hard work and training. For now, you will come here every day until you learn what is happening to the tree. Once you master the skill of listening, I promise you that everything will be simpler and your progress will be much faster. Magic, after all, is a passionate art: The more you learn, the more you want to know."

Dana exchanged a quick glance with Kai; he seemed as fascinated as she was.

"We magicians can see more than other people," the Maestro said. "That is the source of our power. Compared to us, all other creatures are blind to the mysteries of the world."

He said no more and they started back to the Tower, walking so Dana might note landmarks and learn the way back to the tree. They had gone a good way in silence when the Maestro's voice broke into her thoughts. "The forest is yours. You may wander through it whenever you want, to learn the secrets of the world and of life. But listen well: You must never be in the forest once the sun has dipped below the horizon."

Dana would not have considered going out at night, but such a specific prohibition made her curious. She looked at the Maestro quizzically.

"Night is the hour of the wolves," the Lord of the Tower explained, "when they come down from the mountains to hunt. If you value your life, you will not be in the forest then."

Just as he said that, a long, drawn-out howl echoed in the distance.

"You will hear them howl like that every night," he continued. "Yes, at first it is a terrifying sound. For that reason, last night I had to cast a sleep spell on you — you needed to rest. But you must grow used to it — tonight I will not cast the spell. Still, you need not fear," the Maestro said as they walked into the Tower meadow. "The wolves can never reach you in the Tower. In the Tower you will be safe."

Dana looked at Kai, who gave her a reassuring smile.

The sun was setting over the tops of the trees. Dana again saw the figure of Fenris high overhead, outlined between the merlons on the balcony. The wind was blowing his coppery hair and long cape, but the elf stood very straight, as if he were the sentinel of the Tower.

"And there is one more thing to keep in mind," the Maestro said. He came to a halt and looked down at his new pupil sternly. "The first rule of an academy of high sorcery is that never, not for any reason, should an apprentice disobey the Maestro. Do you understand?"

Dana looked up at the tall spire of the Tower and thought of the dwarf, the elf, the tree in the clearing, of all she was going to learn here, and a wave of excitement drowned out any uneasiness at the Maestro's words. "I understand," she said, and a smile tugged at her lips.

Visions

And in the study of magic and the mysteries of the Tower, five years passed.

The five years were busy ones for Dana. As the Maestro had warned her, the study of magic was all-consuming — and indeed it absorbed her completely. Two years after her arrival at the Tower, she mastered all the spells in the Book of Earth and advanced to the second level, exchanging her white tunic for a green one. Only a year and a half later, she took the examination for the Book of Air and won her blue tunic.

And now, another year and a half after that, she woke and stretched in bed, still feeling tired. Last night she had undergone the test for the Book of Water. It had left her exhausted, yet she felt sure she'd passed; and when she sat up and saw the violet tunic lying on the foot of her bed, she was filled with satisfaction. She had worked very hard to earn this honor: She was now a fourth-level apprentice. One more stage and she would be a maga, a full-fledged female sorcerer.

She jumped out of bed to admire the silkiness of the new tunic in the morning light. Even so, she did not dare put it on. On the table was her new manual: the Book of Fire, the last and most difficult of the books of high sorcery.

Still in her nightgown, she went to the window and breathed deeply. Outside, the air was freezing, but the thermal spell that protected the Tower from the assaults of the elements kept her room at a pleasant temperature. She had become so used to the comfortable warmth that anywhere she went, no matter how cold, she would have expected to keep a window open.

Yes, she had changed a lot since her arrival at the academy of high sorcery five years ago. Now she was a young lady of fifteen, tall and serious, and dedicated to magic. She had learned many things at the Tower, but the most important thing was that she had been born for this. She could no longer conceive of a life away from the Tower and her enchantments. Her greatest ambition, although she hadn't told anyone, was someday to surpass the Maestro and become an Archmaga, a high priestess of sorcery.

Archmagi were the only sorcerers higher than Maestros. The Lord of the Tower had dedicated his life to studying and perfecting his magic, and yet he had not achieved that level, which was reserved for only a few chosen practitioners. He was, however, a mentalist, one of the most powerful magicians, because he used his mind to read people's thoughts and influence them. Dana had no way of knowing whether someday she would surpass him, but she worked very hard every day, understanding that was the only way she could achieve her goal.

This morning, however, she intended to take a break.

She smiled and at last changed into her new tunic, shivering as it brushed against her skin. Then she washed her face and used her fingers to comb back her short, rebellious black hair. She had cut off her curls some time ago, finding them a nuisance. Besides, they did not fit the image she wanted to project: that of an apprentice to sorcery who was already quite powerful and who had consecrated her time and life to magic.

That afternoon, Dana took Moonstar out for a gallop. She rode into the forest with the assurance of someone who knew every inch of it, stopping at places that held rich memories, such as the clearing where the Maestro first taught her about magical energy. The tree that had been close to dying years before because of a termite infestation now stood tall and strong.

And the secret was so simple, Dana marveled. *Just blending our energies, feeling what the tree was feeling*. She smiled to herself. Now that seemed like child's play.

She continued through the forest, feeling at ease, enjoying the ride, and occasionally pausing to fill little pouches with some plants Maritta had asked her to bring back and with those she needed for her own potions. She stopped beside a stream, dropping Moonstar's reins so the mare could graze at will, then knelt down to drink. Almost immediately her senses warned her that she was not alone. She looked up, her cool blue eyes scrutinizing the landscape, and relaxed only when she saw a blond youth sitting at the foot of a willow on the far side of the stream.

"I'm happy to see you again," he said with a smile.

"Again? We see each other all the time," she replied.

It was true, up to a point. Kai still lived in the Tower, in the room next to Dana's, but the two had grown apart as she had begun to apply herself almost exclusively to her studies.

"You've been pretty much locked away these past few months," he said. "Too bad you couldn't find some time to spend with me."

"I was studying for my examination," Dana reminded him.

"But now I see you have passed it," Kai observed, nodding at her new tunic. "Congratulations."

He stood up and in two jumps was across the stream and beside her. Dana caught herself admiring the elegance and confidence of his movements, then quickly glanced away. She had promised herself she would never . . .

"Why not take a day off tomorrow?" Kai said. "We'll go exploring, the way we used to at the grange."

"I can't. I've taken a break today, and tomorrow I have to begin the Book of Fire."

She had answered too quickly; he'd know he had the advantage. Indeed Kai lifted his hand and softly stroked her cheek. "Come on, do it for me."

Dana looked into his eyes and saw tenderness there, but also a spark of mischief. She pulled away from him. "I told you, I can't."

Kai tilted his head to one side. "You'll break my heart if you leave me here alone again."

Dana tried to look annoyed, but deep down she knew that she could not resist his spell.

And Kai knew it too.

"Come on, you're a marvelous sorceress," he said. "Surely you can allow yourself one more day of rest. It won't make any difference."

This was true, and Dana had to admit it. Her progress had surprised even the Maestro. But Dana also knew that she had not gotten to where she was with natural talent alone: She had worked very, very hard to reach her present level.

"I'm sorry. Another time." She turned and walked over to Moonstar to signal an end to the conversation.

"I miss you," Kai said very quietly.

Dana asked herself how he could be so cruel. Yes, she missed him too, she admitted reluctantly, but she had to keep her distance. It wasn't just her studies; there was another, more powerful reason, and Kai knew it as well as she.

"Go to the devil." She growled the words more than spoke them.

She grabbed Moonstar's reins. More than anything, she wanted to race back to the Tower, lock herself in her study, and forget everything as she opened the first pages of the Book of Fire.

"That wasn't very nice," Kai remarked. "I'm telling you for your own good — emotions are part of life, and they should not well up inside you only to be pushed down and buried. You need to realize that."

Angrily Dana snapped her fingers, and she and her mare disappeared from the grove, rematerializing far away from Kai. The teletransportation spell was one of the first things she had learned from the Book of Air, and she had mastered it to perfection. She could have reappeared in her room in the Tower, but there was still a little time before the sun dropped below the horizon, and she preferred to end the day with a calming ride home.

How had things with Kai come to such an impasse? Once she had sworn to herself that she would never allow anything to get in the way of her friendship with him. But . . .

Her cheeks flushed when she remembered how she had begun to see something more than a friend in Kai. And how vainly she had fought against that feeling. Pride prevented her from being truthful with him, especially in view of the fact that toying with her seemed to amuse him.

She knew so much more now than when she had arrived at the Tower. She had searched everywhere for information on incorporeal beings, visions as thin as air, with the hope of finding some clue to Kai's nature. Angels, specters, apparitions from other planes, even demons that took on human form, seen only by those they chose to be seen by: None of them seemed to fit Kai, because Kai was changing with the years, aging like a human being. And while immaterial beings could adopt any form they chose, they never did it so naturally, and with such perfection.

Often Dana was convinced that Kai was what her older sister had said he was that long-ago night on the grange: just a product of her imagination. The Maestro sensed her friend's presence, she was sure, but perhaps that was because of his ability to read her thoughts. Perhaps he didn't see Kai directly.

Whatever the case, Dana no longer trusted Kai, at least not in the way she once had. Yet deep down, she knew that her distrust came from fear, fear of the emotion growing inside of her — an emotion evoked by someone she couldn't touch!

"I'll have to have a talk with him," she said to Moonstar. "But whenever I see him lately, he's so sarcastic; I get the feeling that he's mocking me because he knows I . . ."

She stopped. She would never admit it aloud.

"Soon I will be a maga," she told herself. "In one or two years at most. And a maga must be strong and not let anything distract her from what she has to do."

The tall silhouette of the Tower rose before her, and she saw Fenris scanning the horizon from the balcony, as he did every evening. He had passed his Fire examination two years before, so he was now a consecrated sorcerer. His flame-bright tunic stood out against the gray of the Tower like a beacon, or a warning.

Dana had often wondered what he did in the Tower, but she had never made an effort to find out. After five years she still had not gained the elf's confidence; though never unpleasant, he was always cool and reserved with her, and by unspoken agreement, they treated each other with a courtesy bordering on indifference. Most of the time they simply avoided encounters.

When Dana arrived at the enchanted gate, she opened it with a simple incantation. She smiled as she dismounted, remembering the first time she had ridden through that portal, and let Moonstar make his own way to the stable.

Before going up to her room, she stopped in the kitchen. "Good evening, Maritta."

The dwarf replied with a grunt. She was busy putting a bright shine on an ancient stewpot. The dinner pans were piled in the sink, along with the plates and utensils, all of them still unwashed.

"I see you've been working hard today," Dana said, and in a low voice, without waiting for a response, uttered the words of a spell. Immediately, invisible hands began to wash the dirty dishes and pans.

Maritta observed the marvel unfazed. "You ought to save your energy to practice more important things," she muttered.

Dana knew that was Maritta's way of thanking her, so she accepted the gruffness for what it was. "I've brought the things you asked me for," she said, placing several small pouches on the table. "Rosemary, nuts, lavender, chamomile, wild blackberries." Maritta came over to inspect her gatherings.

Dana saw that her meal was waiting on a tray, as it was every evening. Fenris and the Maestro usually transported their meals to their rooms by magic, and never came down to the kitchen. Dana, however, liked to eat in the kitchen and keep Maritta company.

With a glance at the sink, where the dishes were becoming bright and clean, she sat down in front of her steaming plate. But she found she didn't really feel like eating. She poked at a potato distractedly, then methodically began to mash it to bits.

"I didn't know that you had it in for potatoes," commented Maritta. "Aren't you hungry?"

"Not very."

"You had a difficult examination yesterday. I thought you would want to get your strength back."

Dana continued to poke at her potatoes without eating them. She scarcely heard what the dwarf was saying.

"What is it, girl? Woman to woman, I can tell something is wrong. And I think I know what it is. You're in love."

One of the plates by the sink fell to the floor and shattered to pieces.

"Aha!" Maritta exclaimed triumphantly.

Dana groaned and concentrated on restoring the dishwashing spell. When she was sure it was functioning correctly again, she returned to her now flattened potatoes. All her good humor from the afternoon had evaporated. It was not turning out to be the perfect day she'd wanted. First her encounter with Kai, and then such a whopping lapse in a truly simple spell . . .

Maritta watched her for a while. "It's that elf, isn't it?" she said. "He's too much of a string bean for my taste. And the males of his race never grow beards, which doesn't help their looks, in my opinion." She sighed. "But I understand how you might find him attractive."

Dana didn't answer, although she found the dwarf's supposition amusing. Who else could Maritta imagine she'd be interested in? She couldn't see Kai. *No one can see Kai,* she reminded herself bitterly.

"That elf is very conceited," she said in a quiet voice.

"But very handsome," Maritta responded slyly.

Dana didn't contradict her; she wasn't in the mood to argue. When she saw that all the dishes were clean and neatly stacked beside the sink, she got up from the table, said good night, and went to her room.

For a long time Maritta stared at Dana's plate, untouched except for the potatoes she'd mashed into a heap with her fork.

It was hard for Dana to sleep. It wasn't because of the howling of the wolves; she'd grown accustomed to that. Nor was it the wind rattling her window frame.

It was Kai's green eyes, buried in the deepest corner of her heart.

She got up to cast a spell to calm the wind a little. It was a cold night, and the window she opened offered a beautiful view of the valley from the safety of the Tower. Looking out, Dana felt a little more relaxed.

She forced herself to think about what she would be doing from that moment on. Even with the violet tunic, she had a long road to travel before she won the red robe that would mark the end of her apprenticeship. When she passed the Book of Fire examination, she would be a recognized sorcerer, and she could stay in the Tower or go somewhere else to perfect her art still further. She would decide that when the time came. Now she needed to study. Study hard.

Kai had helped her when she was a little girl, but now she wasn't comfortable in his company. He was actually a stumbling block for her, because seeing him even in passing distracted her and kept her from concentrating.

"It is my destiny to be a magician," she said aloud, and her blue eyes grew hard. "If to do that I must go on alone . . . well, so be it. I don't need anyone else. Not anyone." She turned to go to bed; she needed to rest.

Dana didn't know that Kai was sitting in the window seat of the next room, listening to every word.

She woke before sunup. Her subconscious had pulled her from the deepest level of sleep to warn her of a presence nearby. At first she thought it must be Kai, so she was startled when the pale light sifting through the open window revealed a woman standing on the far side of the room.

Dana sat up and lit the magic candle she kept on her bed table. Instinctively she prepared a defensive spell, although something told her she would not need to use it.

The woman smiled warmly. She was not very tall, but she commanded Dana's respect, perhaps because of her golden maga's tunic, or perhaps because of her serene expression and the wisdom in her eyes. Dana judged her to be in her middle years — her dark hair was beginning to turn gray — and found her very beautiful. Her brown eyes studied Dana with understanding, yet Dana knew this woman was not a real person. She was some sort of image: Dana could see right through her.

"Who are you?" Dana asked.

"A prisoner," the woman replied. "Please, look for the unicorn."

"But . . ."

"Look for the unicorn. And do not tell anyone you have seen me."

The image flickered. "The unicorn," the woman repeated before she faded completely.

Dana realized that the woman, whoever she was, could not communicate any longer. She shook her head with amazement. Then suddenly she saw herself running through the forest in the dead of night, fleeing from a pack of growling, howling wolves. Screaming, she ran and ran toward a light beyond the trees. The wolves were right at her heels, but she kept running. . . .

She came to a clearing lit by an enormous bonfire. Fenris and the Maestro had their backs to her and she ran toward them, begging them to help . . . until she saw what they were doing.

They were casting a spell on Kai, transforming him. He cried out in agony as he slowly changed into an enormous gray wolf.

"Kai!" she screamed.

And then the wolf smiled, showing a long row of pointed teeth, and sprang toward her with a savage light sparkling in its green eyes.

"Kai!" Dana shrieked again.

She woke in her bed, shivering and sweating, her heart pounding.

"I'm here, Dana," said a voice by her side.

Dana jerked away from him. But he wasn't a wolf any longer, he was a fifteen-year-old boy sitting beside her, looking very worried and very tender.

"It was a dream, Dana."

She struggled to catch her breath. "You . . . y-y-you . . ." she stammered. "They were transforming you into a . . . and you . . ."

"Don't think about it anymore. All right?"

"All right, but don't leave. Please stay with me tonight."

Kai said nothing, but stretched out next to her on the bed. They lay in silence for a long while.

"There was a woman. She told me . . ."

"It's all right, Dana. It was only a dream."

"No, I'm sure it wasn't a dream. She told me she was a prisoner. She communicated with me and asked me to look for the unicorn."

"She 'communicated' with you? What do you mean?"

"She looked like a maga. I think she must be a very powerful sorcerer. She must have sent her image from wherever it is she's being held prisoner."

"But why to you? Why not to the Maestro?"

"I don't know. But she asked me not to tell anyone."

"You just told me," Kai observed. "So I'm no one?"

In her relief at seeing Kai, Dana had overlooked the woman's request. Now, once again, Kai's sarcasm leaped out, and Dana regretted her impulsive confession. But she was also sorry that the moment in which all barriers had disappeared was over so quickly.

"There are people who don't believe in things they can't see," she said dryly. "For example, you're not anyone to Maritta, and not to most other people, either."

The wounded look on Kai's face made her repent her words. "I'm sorry," she hastened to say. "I didn't mean to hurt you."

"You've been doing that for a while now," he said.

"I said I'm sorry. I . . . I don't know what's happening to me." Suddenly she felt an overpowering desire to make her peace with him, to have things be as simple as they used to be. "Can you forgive me?"

"Can you forgive *me*?" Kai answered after a moment's silence. "I've been behaving very badly, thinking only of myself."

Dana's nerves were tingling. She had never imagined that they could confess such things to each other. All she could think to say was, "Then will we be friends like before?"

"Is that what you want?"

"I don't know. It frightens me. I don't know who you are."

"That didn't use to matter to you."

"But now it does. Now I know a lot more about everything else, but I still don't know anything about you."

"Everything in its time," he whispered, stroking her hair. "Now you need to sleep and rest. And tomorrow we'll look for the unicorn. Isn't that what the woman asked you to do?"

"But she also asked me not to tell anyone. And I can't do anything behind the Maestro's back, Kai. No one can. He knows everything."

"We'll think of something. Good night."

"Good night, Kai," she said. She curled up next to him and closed her eyes. Suddenly everything seemed much simpler.

But Kai lay awake long after Dana fell asleep, sunk in a sadness far greater than she could know.

The next days were busy and confused. In her eagerness to start the Book of Fire, Dana decided not to think about the woman in the gold tunic who had called for her help. She had many things to do, and she didn't want to complicate her life with another one.

But the prisoner did not give up so easily.

She came to Dana many times: in her room, on the stairs, on the terrace, in the library. . . . Often the images of her were crystal clear; at other times Dana could barely discern her outlines. Often she didn't speak, but when she did, it was always the same message: *Look for the unicorn.*

At first Dana tried to ask her for more details, but it seemed that the woman's power was limited; her image was unable to say more. After a while, Dana decided to act as if the woman weren't there. She was tired of seeing things no one else could see.

But with the woman insisting on appearing and disappearing before her, it became more and more difficult to concentrate. One evening she interrupted Dana in her study as she tried to conjure a mischievous fire genie. Dana only just managed to recapture the genie before it could escape and enflame the whole Valley of the Wolves. Finally Dana decided that she would have to do something, and quickly. If she weren't able to keep her mind on her studies, she might even endanger her life.

6
Questions

So Dana buried herself in the library to learn everything she could about unicorns. She gathered a lot of information, but nothing that seemed conclusive. There were so many competing legends she didn't know which ones to believe.

One day she ran into Fenris in the library. The elf magician was in a good humor that morning and smiled at her, so she dared to ask whether he knew anything about unicorns.

"I was wondering how long it would take you to become interested in them," he said.

"Why is that?"

"Because at some moment in their lives, all sorcerers look for a unicorn. It is said that a unicorn's magical horn provides almost limitless power to whoever possesses it."

"*It is said*," Dana repeated thoughtfully. "And is that true or is it a legend? So much has been written about unicorns, I'm sure much of it must be false. How can I know which books are telling the truth and which are merely spinning fairy tales? It's frustrating."

"Searching for a unicorn is in itself frustrating. Many magicians and apprentices before you have tried to capture one with no luck. Some people even believe unicorns are extinct."

"Do you think they are?"

"It's possible. The most widely held opinion is that there are some left, but only a few. They're almost impossible to capture and study."

"Why?"

"Because they are magical creatures, supernatural, wild and free as the wind, and much more intelligent than any mortal. No one can see them unless they allow it." He stared at her intently. "Or perhaps you have come across one?"

"No. Should I have?"

Fenris smiled. "It sometimes happens. So you know this forest inch by inch, but you haven't seen the unicorn in the Valley of the Wolves."

"You mean to tell me that there is a unicorn in *this* forest, the forest of the Valley?"

The elf shook his head. "I wouldn't swear to it. Many legends say so, but to my knowledge no one has ever seen it."

Dana mulled over that new information.

"You can try to find it," Fenris added. "But I'll wager that you won't. I'm almost certain there is nothing in those woods but wolves."

He pronounced the word *wolves* with such bitterness and resentment that it startled Dana; she had never heard Fenris speak in anything but a polite tone. She was curious to know more, but he had gone back to his reading.

Feeling dismissed, Dana picked up her things and started toward the door.

"Good luck," the elf called.

"Thank you," she said, thinking over what he said and wondering how to proceed. The unicorn . . . could the lady be referring to this unicorn, the one in the Valley of the Wolves? In the forest that surrounded the Tower and that she knew so well? How could she hope to find a unicorn that no one had ever seen?

As she climbed the spiral stairway toward her room, the lady in the golden tunic appeared to her once again. Dana was accustomed by now to the image coming and going and usually tried to ignore her. But today she needed more information.

"My lady," she began, "for some time now you have been appearing to me. If you don't want to reveal your name or where you are, at least tell me what I must do. Where am I to look for the unicorn? In this valley?"

The lady gazed at her with great sorrow. "Full moon," she said.

"What does that mean?" Dana asked, but the image vanished as suddenly as it had appeared.

She sensed a presence at her back and turned. The Maestro was standing behind her.

"Good afternoon, Dana. With whom were you speaking? Were you perhaps conjuring? Practicing some invocation?"

Dana did not know what to answer. She nodded but said nothing.

"I am glad to hear you study so constantly," he commented, regarding his student with piercing gray eyes. "How are your exercises progressing?"

"Well. I've begun the Book of Fire, and if I continue at this pace I may be ready to be examined at the end of a year."

The Maestro shook his head. "Too soon."

"I work hard," Dana objected.

"I know. You move forward quickly and you learn well. You are a remarkable student. But you must be fully prepared before your last examination. One does not play with fire."

Dana gave a nod of assent. "Then I should return to my studies," she said, continuing up the spiral stairway.

The Maestro stood watching his pupil. When she was out of sight, the sorcerer permitted himself a brief smile. "Finally, we are getting somewhere," he murmured.

Back in her room, Dana sat by the window to think.

Full moon. Did that mean she would be able to see the unicorn only in the light of a full moon? Dana remembered perfectly how, when she had first arrived, the Maestro had warned her never to leave the Tower at night. "But I was just a little girl back then," she said aloud, "and now I control three elements. I know many spells that would hold off a pack of hungry wolves."

"You could send me to confront them," she heard a low voice say.

"Confront whom?" Dana did not need to turn to know it was Kai.

"The wolves."

Kai joined Dana at the window, and she told him what she'd learned in the library and on the stairs. Instantly a spark glinted in his green eyes, a spark Dana knew very well.

"Great! An adventure! Life around here was getting a little dull. When is the next full moon?"

"Wait a minute, Kai. First of all we should find out who that woman is and where she is sending her messages from. It could be a trap."

"You believe that?" There was a hint of skepticism in Kai's voice.

"I don't, really," Dana admitted. "She doesn't seem evil. But then why did she disappear around the Maestro?"

"When are you going to realize that there is something sinister about your Maestro, Dana?"

"Oh, come on. He's severe, and he doesn't talk much, but he isn't a bad man. He's always been good to me."

"You said he saw you talking with the prisoner's image. Do you think he saw *her*?"

"I have no idea. He seemed to think that she was someone I had invoked, a being from another plane that I'd brought here with an incantation."

"Maybe she is."

"No. I don't do that kind of magic." She said nothing for a moment as questions raced through her mind. "Maybe she lives in one of the other academies of high sorcery. But then why would she be trying to communicate with me?"

"Or it may be that she's someone like me," Kai murmured quietly.

Dana looked quickly at Kai, but his expression told her that he was not prepared to say any more about the subject that so consumed her. Yet his remark seemed too pointed to have been accidental. His image was always much more solid than the lady's; Dana couldn't see any difference between Kai and a real person until she tried to touch him, whereas the prisoner's image was like a mist that she could look right through. But then again, in both cases, Dana seemed to be the only one who could see and hear them.

Were the two of them, Kai and the woman in the golden tunic, products of her imagination? Couldn't she tell the difference between what was real and what wasn't? When you came right down to it, was she crazy?

She fixed her eyes on Kai. "Do you really exist, my friend?" she asked in a whisper.

He smiled. "It depends on what you mean by *exist*. My dear outstanding apprentice sorcerer, let me remind you of the two basic rules of magic: Everything is possible, and things are not always what they seem."

Dana looked away, feeling both confused and annoyed.

"What are you going to do?" Kai asked.

"I don't know." Dana's eyes were lost on some point in the distant mountains. "I want to know more. I want to know if the risks of pursuing what this woman wants are worth it, because it may not be true that there is a unicorn in the forest. And even if there is, if the Maestro hasn't found it, how can I hope to?"

"I don't imagine the lady would be wasting her time asking you to do the impossible," Kai observed.

"Whom can I ask? I'm not supposed to talk to anyone about the lady, and I've already asked Fenris about unicorns. I doubt Maritta knows anything about them. She probably doesn't even believe they exist. 'Those are fairy tales, girl,' she would tell me."

"Then there's no one else in the Tower," said Kai, and Dana turned to look at him.

"What are you getting at?"

Kai did not answer immediately. He was running a

finger over the rough surface of the stone window seat as if it were tremendously entertaining.

"How long has it been since you visited the village?" he finally said.

With a start, Dana realized what her friend was getting at. She had been in that village only once, five years ago, on the day she arrived in the Valley of the Wolves with the Maestro. She remembered, however, that the villagers seemed to shy away from the Maestro then.

"I don't know what kind of reception I would get."

"They are simple people who fear what they don't understand. But I'm sure they wouldn't hurt you."

"They couldn't." Dana smiled. "I am a fourth-level apprentice, remember?"

The next morning she went to the Maestro to ask if she could visit the village. She thought of excuses she could use — that she wanted to get out of the Tower for a while, enjoy a change of scene, take a brief break from her studies — and concentrated on them until she had convinced herself of their truth. And when she went to speak with the Maestro, she let all that float in her consciousness and blot out the mystery of the lady and the unicorn.

The Maestro looked at her a moment before he answered. Dana kept her mind on how much she wanted to have a free day because she was tired — which, in fact, was true.

"You may go if you wish," the magician conceded. "However, do not try to cross through the forest at night. You know already that it is dangerous."

Dana nodded and thanked him profusely.

That night she could scarcely sleep. It was the first time in five years she would be so far from the Tower. She couldn't wait for dawn to come.

By the time she swung up onto Moonstar at the break of day, she had almost forgotten the real purpose of her trip to town. She felt lighter than a summer cloud, and as she trotted through the gate on her mare, she had to repress a desire to sing.

Kai was waiting for her outside, leaning against the wall, arms crossed, in a pose of utter serenity. He could not fool Dana, however; she knew he was as excited as she was.

He jumped up onto Moonstar, taking his old place behind her. She gathered up the reins and prodded the mare forward. It was good to be on the way. Despite the cold and an irritating, icy wind, they chattered and laughed as they rode through the woods, and even Moonstar seemed frisky in the timid rays of the sun.

By midday they had left the forest behind and ridden out into open country. Dana stopped her mare on a slope to admire the landscape. Down in the valley they could see the houses of the town, scattered among the foothills and surrounded by cultivated fields. Behind them rose the imposing gray of the mountain range.

"Isn't it beautiful?" murmured Dana.

Kai smiled. He leaned around her to stroke Moonstar's neck. Then he whispered something into the mare's ear, and suddenly she bolted and went racing down the slope.

Dana had shifted to one side to allow Kai to reach the mare's head, and Moonstar's abrupt movement nearly unseated her. She screamed and grabbed hold of the horse's mane. When she again felt in control, Moonstar was still galloping downhill.

"Are you crazy?" she yelled to Kai. "Why did you do that?"

"Isn't it great?" He gave her a grin.

Soon Dana was grinning too. Yes, it was great. Moonstar was racing like the wind; Dana felt as if she were flying, and everything was much more beautiful with Kai near her. She whooped with joy, and Moonstar answered with a whinny of pleasure. Kai burst out laughing, and Dana joined in.

Coming down toward town, Dana observed everything with interest. They passed farms with herds of cows and flocks of sheep and saw young people working in the fields and children playing in haystacks. Certain images, sounds, and smells brought back memories of the grange to Dana.

"Do you miss it?" asked Kai, divining her thoughts.

Dana squeezed the amulet that her mother had given her, which she always wore around her neck. "In a way I do," she answered. "But I could never live on the grange now that I have known magic. I think, in the Tower, I've found the meaning of my life."

Kai nodded. "You've found your calling."

Dana could not fail to notice that the people she met along the way all looked at her with a mixture of curiosity, respect, and fear. Some gazes held outright distrust, even hostility.

"Simple people do not understand magic," Kai reminded her.

It was early afternoon when they arrived in town. There were not many people in the streets, and Dana wondered whether it was because of her. She decided not to dwell on that but rather to concentrate on what she had come for.

First she went to a herbalist's to buy some medicinal plants that she hadn't been able to find in the forest for Maritta. Then she looked for tools and kitchen utensils. Everywhere she went she was treated politely, though not warmly, but that was what she had expected. Once she had made her purchases, she looked at Kai, a little lost. Where should she start seeking information about the unicorn?

Kai had no more idea than she did. The town plaza was deserted. The only person Dana saw, half-hidden around a corner, was a redheaded boy of nine or ten. She walked toward him. The child backed away, giving her a defiant look.

"I'm not afraid of you," he told her.

She smiled. "And why should you be afraid of me?"

"My mother says you're a witch."

"And what do you say?"

"I don't know. You dress funny, and I've never seen you around here. I think . . ."

"Nicolás!" thundered a woman's voice.

The boy jumped. "My mother," he said. "I have to go. If she sees me talking to you . . ."

"Wait," Dana stopped him. "Do you know anything about a unicorn around here?"

The boy thought for a minute, then he frowned. "That's just an old wives' tale."

"Nicolás!" the voice insisted, and the boy ran a few doors up the street and disappeared into a house. The door slammed behind him.

"An old wives' tale," a voice repeated behind her. "And what do we old women know? Nothing about anything."

Dana half turned and saw an aged woman, tiny and bent, sitting on a bench in the sun. She was surprised that she hadn't noticed her before.

"You're not afraid of me?" Dana asked.

The old woman smiled slyly. "Why should I be? From your voice I can tell that you're no more than a young girl."

Dana noticed an absent look in the woman's eyes and realized that she was blind. She stepped closer to her. "What *do* old women know?" Dana asked softly. "A lot more than young boys, I'm sure."

The old woman smiled again. "You're looking for the unicorn," she said. "I can't imagine why you've come here, then. Everyone knows that it lives in the forest, and that it was in the valley long before any human set foot there. Or at least that is what my mother used to say, and my mother's mother, and her mother before her."

"Is it true that it can be seen only on nights of the full moon?"

"I know nothing about that. They say that unicorns can be seen only by pure young maidens, and then only on certain occasions. But it's possible that in the beauty of the full moon they grow careless."

"The forest is very large," Dana said. "Is there a special place where the unicorn lives?"

"The whole forest is its territory. Neither men nor wolves frighten it, and neither can claim a foot of the forest as long as the unicorn is there."

At the mention of wolves a bolt of fear shot through Dana.

"But you don't have to be afraid," the ancient woman continued. "You're a talented apprentice; otherwise you wouldn't be living in the Tower."

Dana flinched and stammered something.

The woman spoke in a wry tone. "Did you think I didn't recognize you? I remember when you came to town five years ago, accompanied by the old sorcerer. You were no more than a girl then, but I never forget a voice, no matter how much it changes or how many years go by. There is something about each voice — the tone, the accent, something — that makes it like no other."

Dana wondered what the old woman had heard her say five years ago. "What else do you know about the Maestro?" she asked.

The old woman cocked her head to one side. "I know what all the townspeople know. What it knows too," she added, pointing to the shadowy forest in the distance. "And what the wolves know."

"What the wolves . . . ?"

"Who are you talking to?"

Dana whirled around. The boy named Nicolás was watching her from a low window nearby.

"I was talking with . . ." Dana waved toward the bench beneath the tree, but she was left pointing at thin air.

No one was there.

She uttered a soft cry, but saw no sign of the ancient blind woman.

The boy giggled. "I don't believe you're a witch," he said. "I think you're batty, you and that crazy old man who lives in the Tower."

He fell silent as a hand grabbed his shoulder and jerked him away. Dana heard his mother scolding him and in a short while saw her face, pale and serious, at the open window.

"I don't care what it is you do in the Tower," she

called to Dana, "but this is no place for witches. Leave this town, and never come near my son again."

Dana wanted to answer, to defend herself, but she remembered Kai's advice and kept quiet. She rode out of town on Moonstar, more confused and lost than ever. The episode with the old woman had upset her, and the boy's voice echoed relentlessly in her mind: "You're batty, you're batty. . . ."

By the time they reached the Tower at dusk, Kai still hadn't been able to make her smile.

In the days that followed, Dana was distracted, locked in thoughts she didn't share with anyone, not even with Kai. The time of the full moon approached, and she still hadn't decided whether it was worth risking her life for a creature that might not even be real.

What if she *were* crazy and seeing things that didn't exist? What if Kai, the imprisoned lady, and the old woman in the town *were* products of her imagination?

In her studies, her progress was slow; even in performing the simplest spells, she constantly made mistakes. The Maestro noticed but said nothing, and Dana's self-doubt intensified.

The one person who did speak her mind was Maritta. "My girl, I never thought that string-bean elf would wrap you around his little finger like this."

Dana smiled sadly and shook her head. "It doesn't

have anything to do with the elf, Maritta. I've told you that often enough."

The dwarf looked at her curiously. "So it's a more serious problem," she guessed. "Do you want to tell me? I might be able to help."

Dana did not believe that confiding in Maritta would do any good. She trusted her, she truly did, but the dwarves' pragmatism was proverbial. They dug tunnels in rock; they were miners and goldsmiths, as well as fierce warriors. They didn't trust or believe in anything they couldn't see and touch.

In general terms, Maritta fit the patterns of her clan, the oldest on Earth. But then what was she doing in the Tower, so far from her own family? Dana had never asked her directly, although she had always been curious about Maritta's history. Perhaps now was the time.

"What do you really think about magic?" Dana ventured.

Maritta frowned. "Why are you asking me that? You know very well what I think. I don't like it. But you have to take things as they come."

"Then why do you live in the Tower? Why did the Maestro bring you here?"

The dwarf's eyes gleamed fiercely. "I live in the Tower because it is my home," she almost spat. "And that Maestro of yours didn't *bring* me; I was already working here when he arrived. That was long ago, my girl. The old goat was just an inexperienced young kid then."

Dana was surprised. It had never occurred to her that the Tower might have existed before the Maestro.

The dwarf's eyes were still shooting sparks. "But those long-ago times aren't worth remembering," she said brusquely. "And if you don't want to tell me what's bothering you, I won't take offense. I'm used to it, after all. No one tells old Maritta anything."

Dana felt a stab of guilt, although she wasn't sure what she had said that upset Maritta. Perhaps it was what she hadn't said.

"I have visions," she admitted, almost without thinking.

"Visions!" Maritta snorted. "Is that all?"

"Yes, that's 'all,' but it's no small thing," Dana said, trying not to be insulted. "Sometimes I worry that I can't tell the real from the imaginary. And of course I don't know if the imaginary really *is* imaginary or if it's part of a different plane of reality."

She felt as though she had tangled things badly. She looked at Maritta; the dwarf seemed to be thinking hard.

"I don't know whether I'm crazy or whether in fact I can see things others don't see," Dana added, hoping that summed it up.

"I don't know very much about magic," said Maritta at last, "but I have spent nearly a hundred years in this place, and if I've learned anything, it's that when magic is involved, everything is possible. Natural laws are overturned willy-nilly, and nothing is secure or as it was. Everything can be real — or not. Under those circumstances, who's crazy and who isn't? If I were in your shoes, I wouldn't worry about it. If you're going to devote yourself to magic, you have to learn to live with the consequences. And of course, if you *were* crazy, you wouldn't wonder if you were or you weren't. It's my experience that crazy people don't know they're off in the head."

Dana nodded, grateful for the advice. "Then, do you think I should investigate my visions?"

Maritta threw up her hands. "You're curious by nature. Do you think you're really capable of sitting around not looking for answers?"

"No," Dana admitted. "I have to know."

"You see! So why do you ask me? You already know what you're going to do. You've known all along."

Dana smiled, suddenly feeling happy and lighthearted. She planted a kiss on the dwarf's wrinkled cheek and flew up the stairs. By the time she reached her room, she knew she was going to seek answers, and those answers started with finding the unicorn.

Her mind spun with plans. The moon would be full in only a few days, and although she could always wait until the next month, she was suddenly consumed with impatience. With a good stock of spells for attack and defense, the wolves would pose no obstacle to her. Her main problem was how to get out of the Tower at night. The Maestro had expressly forbidden going out at night, and though she didn't understand the purpose of that prohibition, she feared the consequences of disobeying him.

"The most important thing is not to arouse his suspicions," Kai told her when she discussed the problem with him. "If you behave normally, the Maestro won't have reason to read your mind, and if he doesn't, there won't be any problem."

Dana clasped her hands nervously. It was a rather weak plan, but it was all she had. She had to hope that it would work. Thus, during the next few days, she applied herself to her studies with renewed fervor. The Maestro noticed.

"It seems you've started to concentrate again, Dana," he commented. "I'm delighted."

"I had doubts about a few things," she replied, "but now my mind is clear." She was glad she could put it this way — after all, it was the truth. If she had not been sincere, she knew he would perceive it instantly.

"I'm glad to hear it," the Maestro said, and they went on to another subject.

Finally the night of the full moon arrived. During the day, despite her best efforts, Dana could not avoid feeling restless. The Maestro said nothing about it during their lesson, but before it ended, he looked into her eyes a long time.

Dana went back to her room, consumed with worry.

"He knows," she told Kai, and told him what had happened.

"Do you still plan to go tonight?"

Dana nodded weakly.

"You'll suffer the consequences if you get caught," Kai said mercilessly.

"I know," Dana moaned. "But what can I do? If I'm crazy, it doesn't matter what happens to me. And if I'm not, I soon will be if I don't find what's going on around here."

"All right, but it's your responsibility."

Dana turned toward him, incensed. "Whose side are you on? Are you with me or not?"

"Till death and beyond," Kai vowed.

But Dana did not like the words he had chosen.

7
The Night of the Wolves

The full moon was shining brightly over the Valley of the Wolves when Dana met Kai in the stable. They saddled Moonstar in silence. For now, it didn't seem as if they'd been discovered, but Dana knew that they could not risk riding the horse through the garden to the enchanted gate. She chanted an incantation that included Kai and the mare, and in the blink of an eye, the three reappeared in a moonlit clearing in the woods.

Quickly Dana untied one of the pouches that hung from her belt, took some powder from it, and traced a large circle on the ground. She led Kai and Moonstar inside of the circle and whispered the words of a protective enchantment. Then, with her arms outstretched, palms up, she closed her eyes and whirled around like a top, allowing the energy of the earth and moon to flow through her and spill out onto the mare and her friend.

Though they would look just the same to ordinary eyes, they were now surrounded by a spell that would defend them from any possible attack. Dana was pleased.

Almost without pausing, she began a second enchantment, which the Book of Earth called Eyes of the Cat: It would enable her to see in the dark. She knew that torches or any other source of light might reveal their position, and although the moon was full, she needed to perceive even more clearly what was happening around her. Fortunately the spell did not burn up a lot of energy. She would need all her magic that night.

Kai smiled at how amazingly wide his friend's pupils had grown. "What's it like?" he said to her.

"Incredibly better," Dana replied. "I can see outlines, shadows, details . . . even things in the distance. So I'll act as guide. Though I don't know where we're headed — the forest is so large."

"Let's simply keep going until we find the unicorn," suggested Kai.

"And if we don't?"

"Then we'll try again the next full moon, and keep looking until we find it."

Dana nodded, and they climbed back onto Moonstar. The woods were quiet, and the occasional howls of the wolves sounded far away. Even so, Dana dared not lower her guard as they rode through the dense vegetation. She could see better than Moonstar and directed her confidently, though the mare remained nervous and skittish.

"See if you can calm her, Kai," Dana said. The boy patted Moonstar's muscular neck and spoke to her sweetly, and the horse quieted.

"You're a wonder," Dana whispered, and felt the gentle sensation of his arms encircling her. She closed her eyes to relish the feeling before she remembered: *You can't fall in love with someone you can't touch.* So she tried to keep her mind on the unicorn, and to forget that Kai was so close that it made her heart beat faster.

They did not speak again for a long time. The hours went by slowly. As Dana guided her mare through the forest, little by little the two enchantments she was maintaining began to drain her of strength. She knew she needed to stay vigilant, to be alert, but sleep threatened to overtake her.

She was about to ask Kai to talk to her to keep her awake, when Moonstar nickered softly and came to a halt.

"What is it?" Dana murmured, trying to clear her head. Above the distant sound of the wolves, she heard the gurgle of a stream.

The mare pawed the ground with her right hoof. Dana focused her eyes on the underbrush ahead of them. She saw a light in the blackness like a slender shaft of moonlight, and her heart turned over. She trained all her energies on that spot. Suddenly an inexplicable wave of peace and tranquility swept over her, erasing every fear.

"We've found it," she whispered to Kai.

"Are you sure?" Kai too spoke softly.

Dana did not answer. In her five years in the Tower, she had learned to trust her intuition. She dismounted and whispered to Moonstar to wait quietly. The mare flicked her ears in understanding.

"Are you coming?" she asked Kai.

He nodded and got off the horse. They slipped noiselessly through the undergrowth, following the sound of the running water. Dana peered through the bushes. Once again the white shadow caught her eye, and when she turned toward it she felt her heart would burst with joy.

A unicorn stood drinking from the stream. It was as white as the snow or the foam of the sea, not much larger than a pony but infinitely more beautiful and elegant. A soft pearly mane spilled down its long white neck, seeming to reflect the silvery moonlight. Its long leonine tail swished calmly, and the weight of its delicate body was sustained on four fine legs that ended in small cloven hooves, like those of a goat.

Most beautiful of all was its horn. Long and strong, it appeared to be made from filaments of silver, crystal, ivory, dew, and moonlight, twisted and spun to a sparkling point. It glowed softly in the darkness, defying all the shadows of Earth.

The unicorn lifted its head, and Dana saw the short beard that signaled it was male. She was about to point it out to Kai when the creature looked in their direction.

Dana held her breath. The unicorn's enormous eyes

were two bottomless wells filled with a wisdom beyond human grasp. They were charged with understanding, seeming to absorb everything, even her most hidden thoughts and deepest feelings.

"He's seen us," Dana whispered.

At that, the unicorn turned and vanished into the darkness.

"We have to follow him!" She plunged into the stream, not caring that her boots were immediately drenched. Kai followed.

The magical creature moved smoothly and silently through the forest, and they soon picked up the reflection of his white back some distance ahead.

Dana had a sudden intuition. "He's leading us," she told Kai.

"What?"

"He's leading us. If he wanted to escape from us, he could have done so easily. He wants us to follow."

"You think so?"

"If he didn't, why else would he have stood still so long and let us look at him?" She opened a way through the underbrush, her eyes fixed on the white flash. In the excitement of seeing the legendary creature, neither Dana nor Kai heard the howling of the wolves, now chillingly near.

Suddenly the unicorn was gone.

"Where is he?" Kai asked.

Dana scanned the dark, then shook her head. "We've lost him," she muttered, her face grim. She knew her night vision would not last much longer. Before Kai could stop her, she was running through the trees, ignoring his calls and Moonstar's distant, hysterical whinnying. She ran on and on through the thick growth, alert to any silvery spark that might betray the unicorn's presence, disregarding the branches scratching her face, the thorns digging into her knees, the roots reaching out to trip her, until . . . she thought she saw a gleam of bluish light in the distance and streaked toward it.

She came out in a clearing. Trees bordered it on one side. On the other side was a quiet pool formed by a bend in one of the many streams that ran through the forest. Dana realized her error: The flash she had seen was nothing but the reflection of moonlight on the water. Her vision had deceived her, a sure sign that the spell was waning.

Dana leaned over the pond until her fingertips brushed the water, then slapped it in rage. She had been so close!

Now, perhaps for the first time since she'd seen the unicorn, she registered the horrible chorus of howls echoing through the valley and remembered that she had left Kai and Moonstar far behind.

She jumped to her feet, reproaching herself for being so foolhardy. She had to get back before the Eyes of the Cat faded completely. Using as little of her remaining energy as possible, she teletransported herself to the clearing where she had left Moonstar.

The mare wasn't there.

What was there, Dana saw with terrible clarity, was a sea of eyes staring out at her from the darkness. The wolves were larger than she could ever have imagined, and the rough hair on their backs quivered from their barely audible growls. She knew she had very little time. Soon the animals would recover from their confusion at seeing her appear out of nowhere, and then they would not be content merely to bare their teeth from the undergrowth.

She squared her shoulders and gauged the energy emanating from the wolves. To her surprise, it vibrated with something much more menacing than a simple need to eat or to defend their territory. There was rage in the wolves, hatred, fury . . . a mixture of sensations Dana had never believed possible in animals. And she sensed something more, something she could not quite name.

Even though Dana's every instinct shrieked that these wolves were not ordinary, and that she had better escape while she still could, she performed the first of the enchantments she had prepared to ward them off. All she had to do was frighten or distract the wolves long enough to get out of the clearing and look for Kai and Moonstar.

A ball of fire exploded in the air, illuminating the clearing. Fireballs were one of the enchantments in the Book of Fire, though Dana had not yet fully mastered them. This was a smallish one, yet it should have been enough to frighten away the wolves. But when the radiance of the fireball faded, they seemed little affected, and their growling grew only louder and angrier.

Dana was ready with another spell. She shouted words of ancient magic, lifted her arms, and sent energy flowing out through them. A blue wave spread across the clearing at the same instant that a few of the wolves leaped toward her. Those touched by her energy froze in midair.

But the other wolves left Dana no opportunity to congratulate herself. Not in the least intimidated, they advanced toward her with glowing eyes, their hackles raised and lips drawn back over lethal fangs.

Dana was panting now from exhaustion and agitation. One part of her screamed to teletransport herself to a different place, back to the Tower or even to the grange, anywhere far away, but she could not leave her friends behind.

She began to work frantically, casting spells as fast as she could, one after another. Waves of ice, small earthquakes, lightning bolts, tornadoes . . . She turned several wolves to stone and succeeded in invoking a couple of trees to trap others among their branches and roots. Nevertheless, the wolves kept advancing. Dana wondered where they could all be coming from.

Then one of the stone wolves growled.

Dana felt paralyzed with terror as she realized what that meant. There weren't *more* wolves, they were the same ones. After a few minutes, the frozen, burned, or petrified wolves were coming back to life. Her magic was failing, or wasn't strong enough, or . . .

"But that's not possible!" she screamed, continuing to send lightning and waves of ice all around her. And still the wolves kept falling, only to renew their attack moments later.

Dana knew she would have to flee soon, but she refused to abandon Kai and Moonstar in the forest. Kai probably wasn't in danger, but the mare could die.

And, Dana thought to herself, so could she.

Not very far away, high in the Tower, the Maestro stood watching the strange display of flashing lights issuing from some hidden point in the forest. The icy wind flapped his tunic and lashed his face, but he didn't seem to notice. His gray eyes were focused on the spot where he knew his student was fighting for her life.

Fenris stood beside him, his almond-shaped eyes boring into the woods as well. The legendary night vision of elves allowed him to see the bursts of magic more clearly than the Maestro, and although not even he could tell exactly what was happening beneath the shadow of the trees, both could guess.

"She won't make it," said the elf.

The Maestro did not respond but continued to observe the spectacle. At last, with a deep sigh, he turned to Fenris. "Bring her back," he ordered, his voice tinged with regret.

The elf didn't reply. His catlike eyes narrowed to two slits and stared at the Maestro accusingly.

"Is something the matter?" the Maestro asked, as though he didn't know what Fenris was thinking.

"I can't leave here," the elf replied softly. "Not tonight."

A vague smile played across the lips of the aged magician. "Yes, you can. And you have one hour to bring my worrisome apprentice back here to the Tower."

With a slight bow of his head, the elf left the balcony, silent as a shadow. Minutes later, he and Alide, his beautiful chestnut steed, thundered along the road to the forest.

Again the Maestro smiled, pleased by his student's choice. In order to teletransport himself to Dana, Fenris would have needed to see exactly where she was. Conjuring up her image in a magic mirror or crystal ball would have taken great concentration, energy, and precious time that the elf did not have.

Yet the fact that he was using conventional means to reach Dana did not mean that Fenris had not improved upon them. Alide's hooves, enchanted by a spell from the Book of Air, flew faster than the wind.

It would not take the elfin sorcerer long to reach the girl.

Dana heard horse hooves approaching and struggled not to let the sound break her concentration. Her energy was nearly gone; she felt dizzy and weak and on the verge of collapse. The wolves were no more than ten feet away, and her spells would not hold them much longer.

Just as the wolves crouched to spring, Kai and Moonstar burst into the clearing. Kai's green eyes gleamed with determination as his arm reached out for her.

"Grab on!"

Dana knew — and Kai must have known too, she thought — that her fingers would close on air. But her relief at seeing him was so great that instinctively she reached for his hand.

Then she felt a sharp tug and somehow found herself behind him on Moonstar. Yet when she tried to hold on to his waist, she almost lost her balance — Kai was as insubstantial as ever.

She pressed against Moonstar and grabbed the saddle.

"How did you do that?" she asked him. "How were you able to do that?"

"We don't have time for explanations!" Kai threw a quick glance over his shoulder. "Get us out of here!"

Dana followed the direction of his look and tried to clear the fog from her head. The wolves were very close. Quickly, she chanted the words of the teletransportation spell and snapped her fingers.

Nothing happened.

Confused, Dana tried again, and again, her terror mounting.

"What's going on?" she exclaimed. "I can't. . . . I don't have enough energy. . . ."

"Let it go! We'll ride back. But we need light!"

The mare had slowed as soon as they had left the clearing and entered the dense forest. Dana's cat-eye spell had lost its power some time ago, and now Moonstar was plunging through the semidarkness with no reliable guide.

Her teletransportation spell had just proved stunningly ineffective. Could she make any other spells work?

Light. . . . Light was related to the enchantments in the Book of Fire. She reviewed the few she had managed to learn thus far and remembered a possible solution: She could summon a will-o'-the-wisp to guide them back to the Tower in the darkness.

She spoke the words and held her breath. Immediately a flitting sphere of light appeared before her, tiny but intensely brilliant. When she looked hard she could make out the form of a tiny genie blazing inside the sphere.

"To the Tower," Dana commanded.

The will-o'-the-wisp laughed and took the lead. Kai guided the mare behind the small ball of light. Meanwhile the wolves were catching up with them.

Dana turned and cast another spell. Her left hand shone with bluish light. She aimed it toward their closest pursuers, freezing the wolves in a beam of ice. Dana knew that they were not likely to stay frozen for long, but the spell would offer her and Kai a temporary advantage.

She soon found that she had an additional problem. Although creating a will-o'-the-wisp had proved relatively simple, it was not so easy to control the fiery little creature. The tiny genie was flying in the right direction, but she kept bumping into trees and bushes, and everywhere she touched, she left behind a spark that threatened to burst into flames.

Dana knew that a fire in the forest would do irreparable damage to the valley, so she forced herself to pay attention to the will-o'-the-wisp, directing her icy ray at any spot the creature brushed.

It was not easy to tend two spells at once, and she was already near the end of her strength. As she aimed her ice beam forward to extinguish a spark in the bushes, her fatigue made her clumsy, and she grazed the will-o'-the-wisp. That touch was all it took to drop the incandescent creature to the ground, frozen.

Suddenly deprived of light, and with the wolves at her heels, Moonstar reared up with a terrified whinny. Dana and Kai slid off into the undergrowth as the frightened horse plunged into the darkness.

Dana leaped to her feet and quickly raised a protective barrier. It would not last long, but she knew that at least it would gain her a little time. The moonlight filtering through the trees was not sufficient for her to see clearly, though her left hand still emitted a soft bluish light.

She used it to freeze a few of the closest growling wolves. Out of the corner of her eye, she saw that Kai was standing beside her.

"There's nothing we can do about the mare," he whispered. "Try to lift us out of here again."

Dana did so, and again the teletransportation spell failed. "Kai," she said slowly, watching the circle of wolves tighten around them. "We are lost."

He didn't answer. His eyes were fixed on the glinting fangs, but his hand found hers and pressed it. Dana shivered anew at that incorporeal contact.

Two wolves moved forward, and Kai stepped between them and Dana. The gesture touched her, though she couldn't imagine how her immaterial friend planned to protect her.

Suddenly, with a great explosion, an enormous ball of fire appeared — a ball of fire that flew in a zigzag like the will-o'-the-wisp but was far, far stronger. As if it had a mind of its own, it tore from wolf to wolf, igniting everything it touched.

A melodious but powerful voice spoke the words of another enchantment, and what seemed like a pack of enormous dogs appeared out of nowhere and threw themselves at the wolves. In the light of the flames, Dana could see that they weren't really dogs, but ghosts of dogs, frozen shadows with eyes as hot as coals. It was a spell far beyond her abilities, and she looked around to find her rescuer.

Fenris's red tunic blazed beneath the trees, his arms raised high.

Dana ran to stand beside him, and Kai followed.

Fenris lowered his arms, studying the battle between the wolves and the phantasmal dogs. "We need to get out of here," he said. "Run as fast as you can."

"But the dogs will handle the wolves," she objected. Shadow specters were terrible, powerful beings, whatever form they took.

The elf shook his head, and Dana saw a spark of fear in his eyes.

So she turned and took off at a run for the Tower, guessing that Fenris could not perform further magic while he was controlling the ghostly dogs. Her head buzzed with questions, but she just ran, hoping that the nightmare would soon end. Kai kept pace with her, and she knew from the light footsteps behind her that Fenris was following them.

Finally they reached the edge of the woods. Dana saw Alide waiting beside the stream, stomping and pawing the ground, his terrified eyes on the dark forest.

Again they heard the wolves howling, dangerously close.

"The specters didn't finish them off?" Dana asked.

"They only entertained them," said Fenris, and his musical voice sounded hoarser than usual.

Dana looked at him. There was something different

about Fenris just now . . . the yellow glow of his eyes or perhaps his raspy breathing. In her exhaustion, she couldn't figure it out.

Fenris pushed her gently toward the chestnut horse. "Get on. Take Alide and ride back to the Tower," he ordered, his words ending with a kind of grunt.

"You aren't coming?" she asked as she mounted. Kai swung up behind her.

Fenris shook his head. "I'll be all right," he rasped, and again Dana noticed something peculiar about his face. Then he slapped the rump of the horse and Alide shot off toward the Tower.

Dana quickly collected the horse and turned him sharply, unwilling to leave Fenris in danger. But wolves were pouring out of the woods now, swarming toward the spot where he stood, and she realized there was no way she could reach him in time. Alide was foaming and skittish beneath her, so she urged him onto the road and focused on the landscape ahead of her.

She faced a long ride around the woods before she reached the open meadow and the Tower. Still, Alide was galloping, the howls of the wolves were receding, and Fenris had said he would be all right. And Kai was behind her, his incorporeal arms around her waist.

Not so *incorporeal*, she thought suddenly and smiled. She might wonder about a lot of things, but she would never again question Kai's existence. A product of her imagination could not have pulled her up onto Moonstar and rescued her in the clearing. She owed her life to him, and to Fenris as well.

Dana let the intangible contact with Kai flow through her, sweet and warm as a ray of sunlight. She was sure they were safe now, and for the moment she didn't care about the lady or the unicorn or even the reprimand that was sure to come from the Maestro.

Half drowsing, she suddenly realized what it was she had seen on Fenris's face. "I have to tell Maritta that she's wrong," she said to herself. "Elves do grow beards."

In her tranquility, Dana did not hear a howl that drowned out all the others, a howl laden with rage and sadness, rising toward the moon like a desperate prayer.

3
A Few Answers

When Dana awoke, it was late morning. The sun was already high, and the golden rays filtering though the window played with her face and short black curls. She allowed herself to return to reality slowly and lazily. How good it was to be in bed, all warm and comfortable.

And then, all at once, her blue eyes snapped open as she remembered the events of the night before. She jumped out of bed — but a calm voice stopped her.

"Take it easy, my girl. There's no rush."

Dana spun around. The Maestro observed her from the chair, his face very serious. She fell back into bed. The Lord of the Tower knew everything, and she had no doubt that he would punish her for her disobedience.

"We very nearly paid a big price for your little adventure, Dana."

"I'm sorry," she murmured and closed her eyes. Images from the previous night came flooding back: the wolves, the howls, the fire and ice, the shadow specters. . . .

"I do not set these rules at my whim, young lady," the Maestro continued. "I told you that it was dangerous to go into the forest at night. The wolves here are not like other wolves, and not even a talented apprentice like you is their equal."

Dana remembered the spells that hadn't worked. "Magic doesn't affect them," she said. "How can that be?"

"Knowledge comes at the pace of a magician's abilities. You will know the story of the wolves in this valley when you are ready to understand it. For the time being, it should be enough for you to know that you can never conquer them. Perhaps from now on, you will think twice before disobeying me."

The Maestro stood up and walked toward the door.

"Are you going to punish me?" Dana asked. Her tone was wary, contrite.

He gave her a quick glance. "You have already been punished. That was a night you will not easily forget. Nor will you easily forget your remorse for having risked Fenris's life so recklessly."

The elf's name affected Dana like the bite of a lash, flooding her with guilt, as the Maestro had foreseen. He had been forced to race to her rescue in the middle of the night, and . . . was he still in the forest? Still alive?

"How is he?" she asked anxiously.

The Maestro took a moment to respond. "He will recover," he finally said, "although he is extremely tired. It was a very harsh test for him."

The old magician left, and Dana sank back on the pillows. In her arrogance, she had assumed that she would be able to vanquish the wolves of the valley. How stupid she'd been!

Suddenly she remembered Moonstar and leaped from the bed again. Quickly she dressed in her violet tunic, washed her face, and raced down the spiral stairway to the stable. With one glance, her fears evaporated. Her bay mare was standing alongside Alide and Midnight, all three horses calmly eating their oats.

She ran to the mare and talked to her, cleaned her hooves, combed her mane, and curried her. She promised she would bring some sugar as compensation for the scare she'd given her, and with that in mind, she went to the kitchen.

Maritta's wrinkled face beamed with happiness as Dana came in. "Child!" she exclaimed. "My little girl!"

She gave Dana such a hard hug that the girl was afraid she would break in two. It didn't occur to her to complain, however; indeed she was warmed by the dwarf's show of affection.

But the next instant Maritta's expression turned severe. "What a time you gave all of us with your mischief!" Her voice held displeasure, even anger.

"I'm sorry," Dana mumbled. "So someone told you about my escapade last night?"

"'Last night,' she said?" Maritta mocked. "You've been asleep for five days, dear heart."

Dana was speechless.

"Yes," the dwarf assured her, "five days. You had me worried."

"No wonder I'm so hungry!" Dana cast a ravenous look at the tray of freshly baked buns on the table.

Maritta followed her gaze. "Eat," she said, and Dana did not need to be invited twice. "You must have been tired when you got back."

"Tired, no. *Exhausted!* The wolves in the valley are extraordinary! You should have seen them!" Dana spoke between mouthfuls. "I attacked with all the sorcery I knew: fire, ice beams, stone. . . . At first it worked, but then it all fell apart. They kept reviving and coming after me, again and again! And each time there were more!" Dana's eyes grew wide as she described her adventure.

"Was it worth it?" Maritta asked softly.

"What do you mean? Fenris almost died because of me. I don't . . ."

"No, that wasn't what I was asking you."

"I don't understand."

"You must have gone there for a reason. I just want to know if you found what you were looking for."

The image of the unicorn filled Dana's mind, and her

face softened. "Oh, yes," she said. "He was so beautiful. Maritta, if you could only have seen —"

The dwarf gestured impatiently. "*You* saw, and that's what matters."

Dana thought that over. Up till now, no one had asked her the reasons for her disobedience. She realized that, more than any possible punishment, she feared the Maestro would force her to answer one simple question: "Why?" Had the Maestro not asked because he knew everything already? Had he read her thoughts and found out that she'd gone looking for the unicorn because she'd spoken with . . . ?

Dana buried her face in her hands.

"Don't blame yourself, child," said Maritta. "What's done is done."

Dana looked at her friend and suddenly longed from the bottom of her heart to tell her everything. But the dwarf had gone back to her chores and didn't seem to want to continue the conversation.

So Dana told her good-bye, took some sugar from the bowl, and went to the stable. After giving Moonstar his treat, she headed back to the Tower and upstairs. She didn't feel up to facing the Book of Fire just yet, so she sought out Kai in his room.

"Good day, princess," he said, smiling as he saw her come in. "You've been sleeping a long time."

Dana made a face. "That's what Maritta told me. I guess I used up all my energy throwing beams and sparks."

Kai laughed. He was sitting beside the window, and Dana joined him.

"It was worth it, though," she added, remembering Maritta's question. "We found the unicorn."

Kai nodded. "Now we can forget the matter and get on with our lives."

Dana looked at him in amazement. "What are you talking about? We haven't solved the lady's mystery at all!"

She stopped when she saw the severe expression on Kai's face.

"Dana, I know there are a lot of questions to be answered," he told her. "But there's only one way to do that: At the next full moon, go back to look for the unicorn and follow it wherever it wants to take us. And you've seen how dangerous that can be. It's not worth the risk."

Dana listened openmouthed. "What are you saying, Kai? You've always taken risks, you always go all out. You know you don't like leaving things unfinished."

Kai looked at her with a sternness bordering on anger. It was a look Dana had never seen before, and she fell silent.

"Listen carefully," Kai said. "Yes, having adventures is exciting, intense. But nothing — do you hear me? — *nothing* is so exciting that you give up your life for it. *Nothing.* Don't ever forget that."

From the passionate tone of his voice, Dana knew he must have a very good reason for speaking the way he did. Yet something inside her rebelled against his words.

"But I want to know," she protested.

Kai sighed. "So do I," he confessed. "But maybe we will find the answers somewhere else. Right now I want to know what happened to your magic the other night. Didn't you tell me you would be able to stop the wolves?"

"That's what I thought, but . . . those animals are really strange! They seemed almost rational."

"What do you mean?"

"When I measured their energy, I discovered . . . I don't know, a lot more than a simple desire for survival. It was as if they were enraged by something specific. Almost as if they wanted revenge."

"And did your Maestro tell you about that?"

"He says that the wolves of the valley are not ordinary wolves, and that no one can stand up to them. And that was all he was willing to say."

"Maybe Fenris can tell you."

Dana shot him a look of reproach. "I don't think Fenris will want to be reminded, Kai. He risked his life to save me."

"You think so? I had the feeling that he was pretty much in control of the situation."

"It didn't seem that way to me."

"What, you don't remember?"

"Remember what?"

"Well . . . what Fenris was doing. Seriously, didn't you see anything that caught your attention?"

Dana frowned, trying to recall everything that had

happened from the time the elf intervened. He had created a zigzagging ball of fire and called up a group of shadow specters in the form of dogs. They ran to the edge of the woods, where his horse was waiting. He had told her to get on and get out of there. She asked him if he didn't mean to come with her, and he had answered by slapping Alide's rump to send him galloping. By then Dana was too tired and confused to notice anything.

That was all.

"I don't know what you mean. You and I came back to the Tower on Alide, and he stayed behind to act as a guard. I didn't notice anything strange."

"You don't remember," Kai said. "Both of us saw him as you turned Alide, and . . ."

He stared at Dana expectantly, but she did not react.

"You saw it too," Kai insisted.

"Saw what? I'm tired of your riddles!"

After a brief silence, Kai said, "You have lacunae!" His voice held genuine surprise.

"Lacunae?"

"Holes in your memory. How is that possible?" He leaned toward her in concern. "Is that a secondary effect of your magic?"

Dana was bothered by Kai's stare, but what he said worried her even more. She had never heard of such a thing.

"What did I lose?" she wanted to know. "I don't remember anything out of the ordinary."

Kai tilted his head to one side thoughtfully but said nothing.

"*What?*"

"Maybe it's better this way," he murmured, almost to himself. "Maybe it's better. . . ."

"What *are* you saying? Aren't you going to tell me what you know?"

"It's for your own good," Kai explained quickly, when he saw Dana beginning to get angry. "The best thing you can do is forget the whole matter and never go back to the woods at night. It's very likely that the next time you won't be so lucky."

"But —" Dana was truly furious. "You start me off on this adventure and now you say to forget the whole thing? I hate it when you only tell me half the story! What is it that you know and I don't?"

"Now, listen, don't be mad," he said, putting his insubstantial hands on her shoulders. "I know that it's frustrating, but I don't want anything bad to happen to you. I would never forgive myself. The other night you almost died and . . . well, I don't want to have to go through that again."

Kai's look was so intense that it frightened her, and the response from her heart frightened her even more. She glanced away, so confused she could barely recall what they were arguing about.

"I'm going to study," she said abruptly, and pulling away from Kai's hands, she rushed from the room.

* * *

That evening, as the sun was setting behind the mountains, Dana went up the spiral stairway that led to the crenellated balcony. She had been up there several times since her arrival at the Tower, but she had always chosen to go in the morning so she wouldn't run into Fenris.

Today was different.

She paused at the door to the balcony. Though the stairway continued upward, Dana had never gone any farther; the Maestro's private rooms were above, a forbidden place.

Dana opened the door and stepped out onto the cold stone. Fenris was sitting beside the crenellated wall, looking toward the forest. His red tunic fell in pleats to the floor. Every other time she had seen the elf at his post, he had been standing.

He turned toward her, and she stopped, surprised to see him looking so ill. His shoulders were stooped, and his almond-shaped eyes had lost their gleam and were ringed with dark circles.

Dana had never imagined the proud elf could appear so exhausted — so defeated — and she could think of only one thing to say: "I'm sorry."

She spoke the words very quietly, but Fenris heard her. He smiled a wan smile, nodded, and again cast his eyes on the horizon.

"Thank you for saving my life the other night," Dana added.

The elf returned his gaze to her and gave her an appraising look. "You're welcome," he said.

Dana could see that he did not seem disposed to continue, but even so, she felt compelled to say one more thing. "I thought I could handle them. That was foolish on my part, wasn't it?"

Fenris didn't reply, and Dana hung her head. She had come up here hoping for answers, the answers Kai had refused to give her. Now she turned to leave.

"It wasn't," Fenris said.

"Sorry?"

"I said that it wasn't . . . foolish. You couldn't have known that those beasts are not ordinary wolves. Many others have made the same mistake; don't blame yourself."

"But the Maestro said . . ."

"He spends more time not saying things than he does actually speaking. We are all eager to know things."

"Thank you." She truly was grateful for his gentle words. "May I ask you something?"

Fenris smiled. "Could I stop you?" he asked softly.

Dana smiled back. "What happened to you?"

Fenris grimaced, and Dana realized that the mere thought of that night must pain him. She was about to say that she was sorry for asking when a chilling howl rose from the woods, shattering the dusk.

The elf leaped up and fixed his eyes on the place it seemed to come from.

"That sounded awfully close," Dana whispered.

"Yes," was his only reply. He stood for a long while with his eyes on the forest. Dana was surprised by the massive amount of energy she could sense flowing from his body, but she didn't dare break the silence with a question.

They heard another howl, this time farther away. Nevertheless, Fenris scowled.

Silence again fell over the Valley of the Wolves. Minutes later, the elf seemed to relax.

"Were you sending out some kind of bewitchment?" Dana asked.

"You are a very curious girl," he observed.

Dana blushed. "I'm sorry, I . . ."

"Don't apologize. I think I would be curious in your place." He gave her a strange look. "We all have our secrets, don't we?"

Dana could only deflect that question with one of her own. "And what is the secret of the valley's wolves?"

The elf's lips turned up in a slight smile. "You went to the village the other day. Didn't they tell you there?"

"Actually, no one talked to me much at all," she sighed. "Was it me they mistrusted, or do they feel that way about magicians in general?"

"Good question. Maybe someday you will find the answer."

Dana nearly stamped her foot. "Won't anyone here answer my questions?"

Fenris laughed out loud. It was the first time in five years she had heard him laugh.

"That is the fate of an apprentice," the elf said. "No one tells you anything until you are a full-fledged magician. All through your training, you drag around a mountain of unanswered questions."

"But you were an apprentice too, until only a short time ago," she reminded him. "Won't you have a little sympathy for me?"

Fenris bowed his head, smiling. "I'll see what I can do. What do you want to know?"

"What is it about the wolves in this valley?"

"It is said that they are the way they are because of an ancient curse on the valley — maybe also on the Tower — who knows? Those wolves are strange creatures, no doubt about it. The person who bewitched them did a good job."

"This curse . . . does it have something to do with a unicorn?"

"The unicorn again? That's probably only a legend, Dana."

She looked down at the ground so her expression would not betray what she already knew. "And what do the legends say?"

"Well, they say there is a treasure hidden in the forest, and that only the unicorn knows where to find it. But the person who owned the treasure made sure that it was well protected. If the unicorn might be a guide to the treasure, the wolves are some sort of guards on it. It's all just legends, I tell you."

"It can't be just a legend when it's obvious those aren't ordinary wolves," Dana objected. "You yourself said that they're bewitched."

"I can see the wolves. On the other hand, I don't know anyone who has seen the unicorn. That's different — that's the part of the story I consider a legend."

"Very well, let's forget the unicorn and concentrate on the wolves. What more do you know about them?"

But at this the elf's honey-colored eyes flashed dangerously.

"Look, I can answer your questions up to a point," he said. "But there are things that an apprentice simply should not know. And I would be grateful if you wouldn't ask me about the wolves again. I don't like it. Be content with what I've told you, Dana."

He turned his back. Dana did not push her luck. She murmured a good-bye and went back to her room, voices swirling in her head.

"That is the fate of an apprentice." "Nothing is so exciting that you give up your life for it." "The wolves here are not like other wolves, and not even a talented apprentice like you is their equal." "I just want to know if you found what you went looking for?" "Knowledge is something that comes at the pace of a magician's abilities." "I don't want anything bad to happen to you. I would never forgive myself."

Turning over everything that had been said to her, Dana decided she would follow Kai's advice and try to forget the matter . . . but only until she was prepared. Prepared to know. Then she would discover the truth about the unicorn, the lady in the golden tunic, the wolves of the forest, and the curse that cast a gloom over the valley.

9
The Flight

Again they heard the wolves howling, dangerously close.

"The specters didn't finish them off?" Dana asked.

"They only entertained them," said Fenris, and his musical voice sounded hoarser than usual.

Dana looked at him. There was something different about Fenris just now . . . the yellow glow of his eyes or perhaps his raspy breathing. In her exhaustion, she couldn't figure it out.

Fenris pushed her gently toward the chestnut horse. "Get on. Take Alide and ride back to the Tower," he ordered, his words ending with a kind of grunt.

"You aren't coming?" she asked as she mounted. Kai swung up behind her.

Fenris shook his head. "I'll be all right," he rasped, and again Dana noticed something peculiar about his face. Then the elf slapped the rump of his horse and Alide shot off toward the Tower.

Dana quickly collected the horse and turned him sharply, unwilling to leave Fenris in danger. But wolves were pouring out of the woods now, swarming toward the spot where he stood, and she realized there was no way she could reach him in time.

Dana choked back a scream and flung her hands in the air; her nightgown clung to her sweaty skin. Gasping for breath, her heart thudding crazily, she came awake and realized she was not on Alide in the forest but safe in her bed in the Tower.

"It was a dream," she whispered, to calm herself. "Just a dream."

A dream? More like a nightmare of fragments . . . fragments of something that had happened a year ago.

She sat up and tried to breathe normally. For a year, ever since she and Kai had gone out to look for the unicorn, Dana had been concentrating only on her studies in the Book of Fire. But it wasn't easy to act as if nothing had ever happened. She could ignore the visits of the woman in the golden tunic, which came more and more infrequently with time; but she couldn't ignore the feelings the whole matter stirred up in her.

Now she was sixteen, and she was getting ready to take the last examination of her apprenticeship: the Test of Fire. If she passed, she would be a fully qualified sorcerer.

She nodded to herself, clinging to that idea, and fell back into bed, ready to return to sleep. But an insistent little voice planted a question in her mind: "Do elves have beards?"

Dana opened her eyes. What a stupid question. What did it matter? And why had it even occurred to her?

A connection tugged at her — Fenris had been in the dream, and there had been something odd about him. Almost involuntarily, an image from her nightmare floated into her mind — and then suddenly she had a terrifying realization. Her dream wasn't a dream at all. It was a memory she had recovered.

Was that what Kai had seen that night? Was that what she hadn't been able to recall when she woke up days later? Why was she remembering it now, a year afterward? She tried to capture all the details: Fenris's voice, the strange gleam in his eyes, the hair on his face, and . . .

When she had turned Alide, Dana had seen — yes, now it was coming clear — the wolves surrounded Fenris, but made no move to attack him. And the elf — had he been petting them? As if they weren't murderous beasts, but faithful dogs?

A short while later, Dana crept into Kai's room, carrying her candle.

"Kai," she called softly.

He was immediately awake. "Dana? What are you doing here?"

"I had a dream — sort of." She sat on the edge of his bed, trembling with excitement.

"And you came to tell me about it at this hour of the night?" he protested.

"It's important."

"All right." Kai sighed.

So Dana told him everything that she could remember, finishing with the part about the wolves surrounding Fenris like pets. "Is that what you saw that night and what I forgot?" she finished.

Kai's expression had grown more and more somber as Dana told him her dream-memory. Now he could not manage to answer her.

"Fenris has power over the wolves!" Dana concluded triumphantly. "Now I know that it's a special gift of his, not magic that anyone else can learn! If that weren't so, any sorcerer could handle the wolves. Was that what you wanted to hide from me? Why?"

"All right, you win," Kai finally said. "I was afraid, that's all. I knew that you'd want to explore the forest again, once you knew, and . . ."

". . . and if we went with Fenris, and he protected us, we could have a chance," she completed his thought. "But why did you hide that from me?"

"I didn't hide it from you," Kai said defensively. "You're the one who forgot."

"That's true, I did forget. And why? What could have caused . . . ?"

"What? Or *who*?" Kai countered. "I think you already know what I'm talking about."

"The Maestro? Are you telling me that he erased my memory? Why would he do that?"

"I don't know. What I don't understand is why you've remembered it now."

"Enchantments don't last forever. But I still don't understand why the Maestro would *do* that."

"Probably so you wouldn't go back into the forest at night. Perhaps to protect you. It may be that he thought you would never get out alive if you tried again, even with Fenris's help."

"And you thought the same. Which is why you wouldn't answer my questions."

"I want you to understand. I'm not afraid for myself, but you . . ."

"You were trying to protect me."

"You came within a hair of never coming back the last time, Dana. Get that through your stubborn head."

"But I *have* to go again. Don't you understand? Now I am almost a sorceress. If Fenris goes with me, maybe I can find the unicorn again and get to the bottom of this."

Kai looked at her for a long time. Then with a resigned sigh he said, "I don't think anything I say is going to change your mind, is it?"

Dana smiled. "Well, don't worry. First of all I have to talk with Fenris, and then we'll see."

"Are you going to tell him what you've figured out?"

"What choice do I have? For all I know, there's no other way to accomplish what that woman has asked me to do."

"All right, go ahead. And if you go, I'll go with you."

Then, and always, she thought he meant, but he didn't say it. "I better let you get some sleep now. Good night, Kai."

"Good night, Dana."

Days later, Dana invited Fenris to come for a ride with her in the forest.

As they set out, their horses trod the well-worn paths in silence. It had snowed the night before, and a blanket of white covered everything. Neither of them was cold, however; the thermal enchantment from the Book of Fire was a simple one.

When they were far from the Tower, Dana explained to Fenris everything that had happened since the lady in the golden tunic had first appeared in her room. She told him about her communications — what she had asked Dana to do — and about the unicorn. The only thing Dana omitted was the existence of Kai.

"You say you saw the unicorn?" Fenris sounded doubtful.

"I'm telling you the truth. I saw the unicorn, and it is the most beautiful creature on the earth."

The elf looked at her, trying to gauge the truth of her words.

"I believe you did see it," he finally said, "because

otherwise, in view of your experience, you would not be so insistent on going back. Because that *is* what you want, isn't it? We both know that tonight the moon will be full."

"Yes, I want to try again tonight, and I know you can control the wolves in this valley. That's why you spend every evening . . . maybe the nights too . . . up on the balcony, protecting the Tower."

The elf bowed his head, but he didn't deny what she'd said. However, it was clear that he didn't like the subject, so Dana went straight to the point.

"So I want you to come with me tonight to look for the unicorn. I need . . ."

". . . my help in holding off the wolves," Fenris finished for her. "I understand what you're after, but I can't do anything for you. I need some proof that your visions are reliable."

"But it wouldn't hurt you to come with me tonight," she protested. "The wolves don't attack you."

"And who would protect the Tower in the meantime? I'm sorry, but I can't help you. I will not go into the forest again at night, especially on the night of a full moon. That's all I have to say on the matter."

"Well, give me a hand in solving this puzzle, then," Dana said, refusing to give up. "Who do you think the woman is who appears to me in the Tower?"

"I don't know, but by your description she must be an Archmaga. They are the only ones who wear golden tunics."

"Aren't you curious? Wouldn't you like to know who she is, where she comes from, what she wants?"

"I have only your word, Dana. I am not going to risk my life for something that only you can see."

Fenris's words affected Dana more than he could have known.

"No," she murmured. "I understand now. These visions are my curse alone."

She spurred Moonstar and headed toward the heart of the forest.

The elf did not follow her. He calmly returned to the Tower, stabled his horse, and went back to his work in the library. Later he went to his tutorial session with the Maestro in the study.

As Fenris was pursuing questions he had about some enchantments, the aged sorcerer put his own questions to the elf. "She has spoken to you," he remarked. "Do you think she will go out looking for the unicorn again?"

"I don't know," Fenris answered, hesitating. "She seems somewhat obsessed by the subject, although of course I have told her that she cannot count on me." He shook his head. "I had enough the last time."

"You were more than one hour coming back, my dear student," the Lord of the Tower reminded him.

"I know," Fenris replied in a soft whisper.

"At any rate," the Maestro added, "I am curious to know if she is daring enough to risk another search."

At first Fenris said nothing, then he gave a slight bow. "Understood."

Dana was kicking at loose stones, scuffing up clumps of snow, when Kai found her in the forest.

"Blasted elf," she grumbled. "Why won't he cooperate with me? I shouldn't have confided in him; now he'll go tell the Maestro."

"If the Maestro doesn't already know," Kai pointed out glumly.

Dana looked at him. "You think the best thing to do is forget the whole matter, don't you?"

"It seems the safest and most sensible thing to do. If the elf won't help you, you may not survive a second confrontation with the wolves."

Dana sank down in the snow at the foot of a tree. "I wish I had never seen that woman. I don't know what to do."

"I understand how you feel, better than you think I do," Kai said, dropping down beside her. "There still are a lot of pieces that don't fit, and I'm fascinated as well."

"Well, since you seem to know more than I do, why won't you bother to find out more?" she said reproachfully. "Is there some detail you haven't told me?"

"Don't get prickly with me, Dana. I'm not to blame."

"I know that, Kai. But you have to admit that you're always hiding things from me. I don't know why I go on trusting you."

"Because we're friends, no?" His voice was not teasing but utterly serious.

"That's true." Dana spoke softly. "And you are much more than a friend to me. You know that."

"Yes, I know."

Dana did not want to dwell on just how well he might have understood her words; but then he leaned forward and put his hands over hers.

"I only wish things were different," he added, looking into her eyes.

Dana's heart beat faster. He did understand her feelings. "I wish they were too," she said breathlessly. "I wish everyone could see you as well as I see you. I wish I could touch you. . . ."

But then the sound of footsteps crunching on snow caught their attention, and they quickly rose to see who approached.

Fenris strolled into the clearing. His red tunic stood out brightly against the white snow. Dana hoped that he had just materialized from the Tower, but from the expression on his face, she guessed that he had been listening for quite some time.

"You were spying on me," she said.

"Who is Kai?" the elf asked, ignoring her accusation. He saw her quickly shift her glance as if someone or something were there, but he saw only empty space.

"None of your business. Go away!" Dana demanded.

"Very well. But first there is something you may want to know."

"I don't want to know anything. Leave me alone. You have no right. . . ."

"Did you know that *kai* is a word in our elf language?"

That brought Dana up short. She looked at Kai. He was staring at the elf with a hard expression on his face.

"I see you didn't know that," Fenris remarked. "Well, if you are interested, it means 'companion.' Some magicians use that word to refer to . . ."

"No!" yelled Kai, beside himself.

"I don't want to know!" Dana cut the elf off. "Please, Fenris, don't say any more. He doesn't want you to tell me."

"And I know very well why," the elf murmured. "All right. I shouldn't stick my nose into things that don't concern me."

"Well, you just did," Kai snapped.

"But you were talking with someone just now? Someone I cannot see?"

Dana looked from one to the other, torn between the desire to know more about her childhood companion and Kai's obvious reluctance for her to find out. "His name is Kai," she admitted at last.

"I see," Fenris replied. "And that brings me to a few disturbing questions."

In one fluid, elegant line, he walked toward her and

sat down. Fenris moved with the flexibility and subtlety of a cat, something Dana had never noticed before.

"That woman whom you see, the one who talks to you, is she like Kai?" the elf asked.

Dana smoothed her hair nervously as she sat down too. She wasn't used to talking about Kai. Even though she had wanted to have such a conversation for a very long time, now it felt like her privacy was being invaded. Kai crouched stony-faced beside her.

"I don't know," she finally answered. "The image of the lady is sometimes so misty that I can see right through her. On the other hand, Kai is as clear and as real to me as you are this minute."

Fenris nodded thoughtfully.

Dana found herself waiting, hoping that he would tell her once and for all what was going on. But at the same time she was almost afraid to know the secret of Kai's nature, the secret he had guarded so jealously for so many years, that had caused her so much pain. . . .

Kai doesn't want me to know, she reminded herself. *He would be unhappy if I found out.* Just as she was going to tell Fenris that she didn't want him to tell her any more, he spoke.

"*Kin-Shannay*," he said.

"*Kin-Shannay*?" Dana repeated. "What is that?"

"That's what we elves call people like you."

The sorcerer fixed his almond-shaped eyes on Dana's, and in them she could glimpse respect, even admiration.

It frightened her, and she returned a look filled with doubt and uncertainty.

"*Kin-Shannay*," the elf said once more. "They are extraordinary beings. In all the world there are only a handful of them. Their powers can become nearly limitless, because they see the beyond; their vision reaches much farther than that of other mortals. They are like a door open to another dimension."

"You're teasing me." She was trembling violently.

"I assure you I am not." Fenris's eyes were still studying Dana. "Now I begin to understand why the Maestro brought you to the Tower."

"*I* don't understand at all!" Dana burst out. "I don't know what you mean! I've never heard of *Kin-Shannay*!"

"I can't tell you any more without revealing Kai's secret, and it is obvious that he doesn't want me to tell you."

"Can you see him even a little?" Dana asked tensely.

"No, but you've made his feelings plain."

The elf lapsed into a thoughtful silence. Dana reached out for Kai's incorporeal hand.

"He brought me to gain access to the Tower, which was besieged by the wolves," Fenris muttered. "But you? Why did he bring you? The key is in that sorceress who talks with you. Haven't you ever asked her name?"

"Many times. But she never answers."

"She is connected with the Tower, I'm sure. Perhaps she lived there a long time ago. In any case, I don't believe I know anything about her."

"Maybe Maritta knows," Dana said suddenly. And when she saw Fenris looked a little confused, she explained, "Maritta, the dwarf in the kitchen. She told me that she lived here long before you and the Maestro arrived."

"Yes," said Fenris, "go talk with her now. And when you come back, bring our horses and some provisions."

"Horses and provisions? What for?"

"To look for the unicorn tonight. I'll stay here because I have something to do, but I will expect you at dusk."

"You're coming with me?" Dana exclaimed. Impulsively she threw her arms around him. "Oh, you don't know how grateful I am! You will leave the Tower unguarded to come with me?"

"What else can I do? I suppose that as soon as the Maestro notices that the wolves are too close, he will realize I'm not there and come looking for us. But in the meantime . . ."

"Wonderful! Then I'll talk with Maritta and we'll meet back here at sunset. Thank you again!" She gave him another hug, then got up, climbed onto Moonstar, and rode off from the clearing, Kai close behind her in the saddle.

By the time Dana reached the Tower, she had managed to turn her mind away from all the comments about Kai and *Kin-Shannay*, whatever those might be. She didn't want to think about any of it. The most important thing now was to find out about the lady in the golden tunic.

Maritta was filling water buckets on the terrace. Dana hurried to give her a hand, Kai close behind. She didn't ask any questions until they got to the kitchen.

"I need your help, Maritta," she said then.

The dwarf's eyes turned on Dana, dark and penetrating. "If it's in my power, I will give it. Tell me, what do you need?"

Dana told her about the visitations from the lady in the golden tunic, describing the woman's appearance as fully as she could. "I know you don't like to talk about your early days in the tower," Dana said, "but maybe if she once lived here you would remember her. . . ."

The dwarf's face had become pale as wax.

"You can't have seen her," she muttered. "She . . ."

"You know her?" Dana asked eagerly.

Maritta's eyes were shining. "When I was young — and that was many years ago — the Tower was a center of wisdom and learning, and travelers and scholars came to her from all parts of the world. This place was filled with laughter and good feeling, and the wolves didn't howl with rage from the mountains.

"Everything revolved around her — the Lady of the Tower," she continued. "The most powerful sorceress in the seven kingdoms, the wisest, the most fair, the most prudent. Everyone in the Tower and the valley loved and respected her. Her name was Aonia."

"And where did she go?"

"Where did she go? To the place no one returns

from." Maritta shook her head sadly. "She died more than fifty years ago."

Those words were a blow to Dana. She had thought she had the answer! But someone who had died couldn't be held prisoner, and the dead did not communicate with humans except when they were summoned by a sorcerer of great power. Her vision must be of someone else. "I understand," she murmured. "I will keep looking. Thank you anyway."

She said good-bye to the dwarf and left the kitchen. As she climbed the stairs to her room, her thoughts turned to her plans for the night. Just remembering her previous experience with the wolves chilled her, but she told herself it would be different this time, because Fenris would be with her.

Why had the elf changed his mind?

"If you go off again, the Maestro might not let you come back," Kai said.

Dana jumped. She had almost forgotten that he was with her.

"I know," she replied. "But it's worth the risk to find the unicorn and discover who that woman is."

Kai said nothing.

"You know," she said, reading his expression. "All of you know — except me. Why can't . . ."

She stopped suddenly. "Maybe she's someone like me," Kai had said once. And that would explain why only

Dana could see her. . . . "It *is* Aonia," she said in a low voice. "The Lady of the Tower."

Again Kai said nothing.

Dana dropped down on her bed. . . . *Kin-Shannay. Kin-Shannay.* That one important word was echoing in her head. She buried her face in the pillow and closed her eyes, trying not to think what it meant that she could speak with the dead. But then she felt the ineffable touch of Kai's hand upon her shoulder, and it sent a chill through her.

"Then you . . ." she said, turning to look at him.

The suffering in her friend's eyes made Dana realize how trivial her own sorrow was.

"You . . . are . . ." she started, trembling, but again fell mute.

"A ghost," Kai finished, his eyes filled with tears.

Dana had never seen him cry. She felt as if her heart would break. "I . . . I have something to tell you," she said. "I am frightened, I am very frightened, by everything that is happening. But what I am most afraid of, now that I know what I know" — her voice dropped to a barely audible whisper — "is what I feel for you."

Kai said nothing, but put his arms around her. "Forgive me," he whispered in her ear.

"Why? For not telling me the truth?"

"No, for loving you. I shouldn't have, don't you see? All I've done is cause you problems."

Dana pulled away to look at him. "Don't be foolish.

You are . . . you are the person I love most in the world. You have given me so much. I don't know what I would do without you."

"There's more I have to tell you —"

"Tomorrow," she broke in, and both of them were silent, realizing all that *tomorrow* implied.

Shortly before dusk, the two friends left the Tower, riding Alide and Moonstar. Dana chanted the magical words to teletransport them to the clearing where she and Fenris had agreed to meet. The Tower was not visible from the clearing, but Dana knew exactly where it was, and she knew that a pair of stony gray eyes might right now be scanning the forest from on high.

Fear stabbed her. Maybe she would never return to the Tower. Maybe she would die that very night. Or maybe the Maestro would kill her with his own hands. She remembered the primary rule of an academy of high sorcery: Never, not for any reason, should an apprentice disobey the Maestro.

Fenris was already in the clearing, sitting on the ground in the snow, in the middle of a circle outlined by various plants, stones, and magical powders. His eyes were closed, and he wore only a loincloth. His red tunic hung from a tree branch. What most captured Dana's attention, however, was the expression of peace and calm on the elf's angular, eternally young face.

"It's a circle of purification," she explained to Kai, speaking very softly. "It's to cleanse oneself of evil spirits."

"Like me?" he joked, but Dana shot him a stern look. "Don't joke about serious things."

"You're right. Sorry."

She sat down and waited in nervous silence for Fenris to finish. Dusk was gathering, and she knew that the Maestro would discover their flight as soon as the elf failed to appear on the crenellated balcony. But she also knew that if Fenris were carrying out a circle of purification, he had his reasons. She ought not to hurry him.

As the first stars twinkled in the sky, the wolves began to howl. Fenris opened his eyes and smiled at Dana. He looked almost comical, sitting half-naked in the snow with a pleasant expression on his face, but his delicate features radiated a profound peace and inner harmony that were irresistibly contagious.

Dana smiled back. *I must ask him how he performs that spell,* she thought. The circle of purification was outlined in the Book of Air. She had used it once to relax herself, but never with such spectacular results.

Fenris got up and stepped outside the circle to reclaim his tunic, casting a quick glance at the sky. "We don't have much time," he said to her. "You take the lead."

Dana nodded, filling her lungs with cold air. She knew the truly dangerous part was beginning now, and whether she survived or not, whether she made it back to the

Tower or ran away, she would never again be the same. Tonight would change her forever.

No matter. She spoke the words of teletransportation that would carry her to the place where she had seen the unicorn a year ago. Instantly, Dana, Kai, the elf magus, and the two horses disappeared from the clearing. Only the fresh remains of the circle of purification bore witness that anyone had ever been there.

10
The Refuge in the Forest

Everything was topsy-turvy on the lowest floor of the Tower. Maritta had decided to scour the kitchen from top to bottom, even though it was nighttime and she had cleaned the kitchen only a few days ago. But she knew she would find it impossible to sleep, and work would keep her from thinking.

Dana's supper was on the table, untouched. Maritta had suspected that the girl would not come down to eat, but she had prepared the meal in hopes that Dana would change her mind. No such luck.

Huffing and puffing, she stuck her head back into the cupboard she was scrubbing. Up in the Tower, the elf hadn't eaten either. He was with Dana, Maritta guessed, and she couldn't decide if that was a good or a bad sign. She had never trusted that skinny creature with the cat eyes.

A sudden howl rent the silence, making Maritta jump.

It sounded far too close, but she shook off her apprehension and busied herself with her scrubbing. A short while later, she felt a presence behind her. She wanted it to be Dana, but knew very well that it wasn't.

"Good evening," came the serene, well-modulated voice of the Lord of the Tower.

"Good evening, sir," Maritta replied, scrambling to her feet.

Differences in height had never intimidated her. Although very few dwarves were even four feet tall, most were stronger than any elves and more than a match for ordinary-size humans. Maritta belonged to an ancient, proud, courageous people — the heroes of many epic legends. She knew that even though she was a woman, physically she could overpower the aged Maestro looming before her.

There was one sphere, however, where dwarves feared to enter: the world of magic. That was why Maritta began to tremble as the shadow of the sorcerer spread across the room, and why she lowered her eyes, not daring to meet his.

The Maestro never appeared in that part of the Tower. The last time Maritta had seen him had been on the day he arrived, nearly half a century ago. She remembered how the magus, then young and strong, with the cat-eyed elf in tow, had ridden up to take over the Tower, which had been deserted since the curse fell upon it. The young man had been surprised to find her there, but she had assured him that she wouldn't make any trouble: She had worked for the former inhabitants of the Tower, and she would continue to work for him.

The Maestro was agreeable. He simply told her never to come up to his rooms and never to touch magical objects if she wanted to avoid disaster. That was no problem for Maritta, so she never had any difficulty with the new Lord of the Tower. Which undoubtedly was why he had never again set foot in her kitchen.

What was he doing here now?

"Fenris and Dana are out," he said. "You know where they have gone."

"And you as well," Maritta replied, with no change of expression.

The magus frowned and gave her a sour look; she returned a serene and resolute gaze.

"You are right," he admitted. "I know where they have gone."

"So, what do you want of me?"

A triumphal howl echoed through the trees. Several other wolves yowled victoriously in answer.

"The wolves are coming," said the Maestro. "And now there is nothing that can stop them. We must abandon the Tower."

"Abandon? And where . . ."

"You once told me that you would always be faithful to the Tower and everyone in it," the Maestro declared. "It is time for you to prove that, Maritta."

* * *

Dana, Fenris, and Kai waited for the unicorn by the stream. In the night sky, the full moon shone in all its splendor.

Dana studied Fenris with concern. He was bent over and having difficulty breathing, and his good humor was fading by the minute, giving way to an apparent internal struggle.

"You must be ill," she said.

"I was born ill," the elf returned.

Though burning with curiosity, she did not ask any more questions. She simply watched as Fenris moved from one dark area beneath the trees to another — anywhere the moonlight couldn't reach him. She heard his breathing getting rougher and more rapid; she didn't want to look at him for fear of what she might see.

Kai, however, observed the magus closely. He poked Dana gently in the ribs. "Look at him," he whispered.

Dana's eyes met Fenris's, and in them she saw the strange gleam — a gleam she had seen once before — of a creature able to see in the dark: a yellowish glint, deep, primitive, and savage.

"I hope the unicorn will appear soon," Fenris said in a voice deeper and more grave than usual.

"Is there anything I can do to help you?" asked Dana. Now she couldn't take her eyes off him.

He shook his head. "There is only one thing you can

do for me. If the moment comes when you look into my eyes and you no longer recognize me, leave immediately. Do not try to escape by running, because you will never succeed that way. Teletransport yourself to a safe place where I can't reach you."

"How can you ask me to leave you behind?" she replied.

"If you don't, you will not get out of this alive, Dana. But it will be some time before anything happens," Fenris added, seeing her tremble. "I have done all that I can. The circle of purification does not make me immune to the effects of the full moon, but it does delay them."

Dana moved closer to Kai. He slipped his arm around her, but despite his delicate touch, she still was uneasy. Who *were* these friends of hers?

The howling of the wolves continued, coming closer. Dana raised her head, trying to calculate how long it would take the animals to reach them.

"Don't be afraid of them," said Fenris, noticing where she was looking. "There has to be some advantage to having me here, no?" He tried to smile, but his mouth twisted into a sarcastic grin.

A soft movement came from the foliage. The three friends quickly looked around. Standing beside the stream, regarding them with eyes deep as the sea and brilliant as stars, was the unicorn. Dana felt her own eyes fill with tears. Kai remained still as a statue, and for a moment,

Fenris ceased to breathe. No one dared say anything, until the unicorn lowered his delicate head, turned, and slowly walked away.

"He wants us to follow," Dana said as she started after him. *And this time I'm not going to lose sight of him*, she added to herself. Leading Alide and Moonstar by the reins, the three quietly crossed the stream and began to trail the splendid creature.

The light from his horn guided them through the dark like a glowing sword. The animal moved gracefully through the snow-covered thickets, his small cloven hooves hardly touching the ground. Three times Dana tried to get closer, and three times the unicorn sped up to maintain the distance between them. Dana finally restrained herself.

"I can feel the wolves surrounding us," Fenris announced abruptly.

His words ended in a guttural noise that startled Dana, who had been feeling an enormous peace as she concentrated on the unicorn's light. "Are you sure you're all right?" she asked.

"For the moment. Let's keep on."

The woods opened onto a large clearing illuminated by moonlight. Up to this point, Dana had known the way, but now she couldn't guess where the unicorn might be taking them.

Suddenly Fenris uttered a low, unmistakable growl. The light of the moon shone in his yellow eyes.

"What is it?" Dana whispered.

She soon saw: Tens of pairs of eyes were watching them from the darkness. Moonstar whinnied, terrified, and Kai hastened to calm her.

The unicorn walked on, but Dana had to stop. The wolves had grown bold enough to show themselves within the area illuminated by the soft radiance of the magical horn. They stood there growling quietly, their hair bristling.

"Fenris?" Dana whispered.

Her legs were trembling; the unicorn was moving away, yet she didn't dare go any farther. She tried to catch Kai's eye, but he was occupied with the agitated horses.

"Keep going." The elf's voice was low and close. "Don't be afraid."

With a light, elegant step, the unicorn walked right past the wolves. There was no change in their growling; they even seemed to ignore the unicorn in favor of Dana and Fenris.

Dana forced herself to follow. She was cold with fear, but she knew she mustn't let the unicorn out of her sight. Suddenly one of the wolves darted toward her, and she screamed.

In a flash Fenris stepped in front of Dana and growled, revealing shining fangs. The animal moaned, backed away, and fled with its tail between its legs.

Fenris threw back his head and howled at the moon. The wolves echoed his savage cry. Then they ceased their growling and even moved aside to let them pass. The three followed the unicorn, the wolves trailing at a cautious distance.

"They're waiting for something," whispered Kai. "Keep an eye on Fenris, Dana. I'm afraid the pack will soon have a new leader to obey."

Dana nodded and hurried along. A short while later she heard Fenris say her name in a hoarse whisper.

She turned and had to choke back a scream. The elf's face was covered with hair all the way to the tips of his ears. His jaw had become long and snoutlike, and he was bent over, moving almost on all fours.

"Get the horses and ride," Fenris ordered.

"I'm not going to leave you here!" Dana objected despite her horror.

"Do what I say!" His command ended with a drawn-out howl that set the other wolves to howling restlessly.

Dana insisted no longer. She jumped onto Moonstar; Kai was already on Alide, the horse shifting under his supernatural presence.

"Let's go!" he yelled, and Dana dug her heels into Moonstar's flanks. The mare burst into a gallop, and she heard Kai and Alide pound along behind them.

The unicorn also set off at a fleet pace, streaking like a silver flame through the woods.

Dana looked back only once. Fenris stood in the middle of the clearing with his glowing eyes fixed on them. Though there was little that was human left in his face, he still held the wolves around him, preventing them from chasing after the fleeing pair.

Dana urged Moonstar on. Kai, now in the lead, pushed Alide to a faster pace. The light from the unicorn guided them through the night.

Suddenly they heard a bloodcurdling howl that eclipsed all the others.

"There's nothing to hold them back now!" yelled Kai.

Dana kept her eyes on the unicorn's glow, wishing with all her heart that they would soon reach the place the magical creature was taking them.

Despite the lead Fenris had provided, Dana and Kai soon heard the wolves' howls getting nearer. Dana spurred the terrorized Moonstar on, but close behind her she could sense the presence of the gray wolves and their new and monstrous leader.

"Faster!" cried Kai, but they both knew they couldn't thread their way through the woods any faster, lest they risk their horses stumbling. Besides, they could go no faster than the unicorn was leading them.

Dana turned in the saddle and shouted the words of an enchantment. Instantly, a glittering wall of ice rose up, and a heavy, hairy body thudded hard against it. Through the ice she glimpsed a creature clawing the wall and howling with rage. It would slow the wolves for a moment, but only as long as it took them to run along the wall and find its ends.

And then a cry of surprise escaped her. The light of

the unicorn had disappeared. Kai too was disoriented, until he saw a low wooden building in the shadows.

"The hunters' lodge," he cried. It was a place Dana and Kai had discovered long ago during one of their excursions in the woods, but they had never been able to find it again. Once it had been used by hunters, but because of the wolves and the valley's mysterious curse, it had fallen into ruin from disuse.

A few seconds later, the two horses thundered across the threshold of the large wooden building. A ramshackle door hung to one side from a single hinge.

Darkness.

"Where did the unicorn go?" Dana asked.

They had no time to wonder: In minutes the wolves would be at the useless door. Dana dismounted and got to work, illuminating the interior of the old building with magical fires. Then she went outside.

When she came back in, Kai looked through the window. "What did you do?" he asked. "I don't see anything different."

Before Dana could answer, a creaking noise began outside. Soon they heard more creaking and scratching, and Kai had the sensation that the whole lodge was moving. He looked at the window again and saw something that resembled a serpent crawling up the broken frame.

"Tell me what you did," he said.

More serpent shapes slithered up the walls of the lodge, inside and out, interweaving with one another, strengthening the worm-eaten walls. Kai studied them more closely and realized they were not snakes but saplings, growing at a dizzying speed.

"I made a barrier of trees," Dana told him. "When the saplings reach full growth, the wolves will not be able to penetrate it. We'll be safe here until dawn, when Fenris will be an elf again and help us."

Kai nodded in admiration.

The wolves soon arrived and began to claw at the magical wall, trying to find a crevice they could squeeze through. Dana paid no attention. She sat down in a damp corner, leaned her head back against the wall of tree trunks, and closed her eyes.

"We've lost the unicorn. What did we do wrong this time?"

"I would guess that we're where the unicorn wanted us to be, although I'm not entirely sure why." Kai sat down beside her, and Dana settled against him, ignoring the growling outside.

He looked at her for a moment and then said softly, "I know you're tired, but I'm going to tell you a story. Will you listen?"

Dana nodded.

"More than fifteen hundred years ago," Kai began, "many dragons roamed the earth. Often they settled in mountain caves near villages, in order to be able to raid the villages whenever they wanted. Once a small but ferocious blue dragon took possession of a cavern in the hills near where you were born. It wrought great havoc and killed many people, but no one came along to challenge it; all the heroes had better things to do.

"Then a rash young farm boy decided it was time that someone did something; so he went in pursuit of the dragon, armed only with two knives dipped in poison, and no protection other than that.

"He found the dragon ravaging a herd of cows, enjoying a fine feast. The dragon knew the lad would be a delicious tidbit compared to the cows, but since it was already full, the dragon decided to leave him for later. When the young farmer boy called out his challenge, the dragon burst into gales of laughter."

Kai paused, a somber look on this face.

"I said, didn't I, that the dragon wasn't very large. Well, compared to others of its breed, that was true. But even so, it measured about twenty-one feet long and nine feet high, with deadly claws and teeth like daggers. Fire spewed from its nostrils. Though it was small, it was both very intelligent and very evil.

"No, the farm boy was definitely no match for this dragon. He quickly lost his knife, and the battle was short and disastrous. The blue dragon didn't kill the boy, it just left him unconscious, planning to carry him back to its lair later, where it would toy with him a while. So when the boy regained consciousness, he found himself high above the ground, clasped in one of the blue dragon's claws. It was flying back to its cavern, very pleased with its trophy.

"The boy thought he might have one chance. Because the dragon flew with its claws tucked into its body, he had a close-up view of its sapphire-colored scales. Moving very slowly, so the dragon wouldn't sense anything, he pulled his second knife from his boot and searched for an opening among the scales. When he found one, he sank the knife into the creature's flesh. The dragon reacted to the pain by opening its claws."

Kai stopped abruptly. Dana felt her heart stutter, but not because of the growling and clawing of the wolves surrounding the lodge.

"I fell from a height of a thousand feet," Kai said at last. "My last thought was, *If only . . . if only I hadn't been so stupid.* And I learned, too late, that life is too precious to take risks without a very good reason."

"It *was* a good reason," Dana commented, but Kai gave her a terrible look.

"You don't know what you're saying. People don't know what they have until they lose it."

After an uncomfortable silence, Kai continued, "They found my body crushed and bruised, and they buried me right where I fell. A hundred years later your ancestors came along and built their grange on that very spot." He smiled. "If one day you go back home and dig at the west wall of the barn, beneath the window . . . you will undoubtedly find my bones. That is, if the dogs haven't dug them up," he finished bitterly.

"Don't say such things," Dana begged him. "Not in that way."

Kai gave her a tender smile. "My soul has been on the Other Side all this time, in the dimension where disembodied ghosts dwell — until I was called and given a mission."

Dana sat up and looked at him quizzically.

"It's fine, really, on the Other Side," he explained. "You could say that we are happy; in that dimension, time and space don't exist, and as we are not bound by physical laws, all things are possible. But many of us have never forgotten the world of the living: There's something powerful and beautiful about life on Earth that can't be found anywhere else.

"What the elf told you is true. Sometimes a person is born who has special powers in regard to us. . . . A person whose mind acts like a door that opens wide between both dimensions, who is able to see us and understand us — who offers us a link with the world of the living. The elves call such people *Kin-Shannay*, which means 'portals.' As Fenris said, there are only a few *Kin-Shannay* scattered throughout the world, and so we try to protect them and help direct them through life.

"By coincidence a *Kin-Shannay* had been born in the village where I lived my brief life. So I was chosen to guide and protect you, to be your *Kai*, your companion. They gave me the opportunity to live again the life I had lived, for as many years as I had lived up to the moment of my death. I could see and feel and talk like a human being . . . with the one exception that I would not have a physical body, and that only you could see and hear me. My mission would be to see that everything went well for you, and that you met no harm. And although that is difficult to do when you are a ghost with no body, and you have lost many of the powers you possessed on the Other Side, I accepted immediately. I had died very young. I was still in love with life. I was willing to give anything to see the sun again, the sky, the trees, people . . . even though they couldn't see me."

"And you came to me," said Dana, remembering their first meeting.

"My spirit returned to the world of the living the day you were born. I spent six years observing you in silence, until one day I decided to speak to you. But I would not be with you now had it not been for the Maestro. My soul would have remained bound to the grange if, on the night you left, he hadn't allowed me to come with you to the Tower."

"Then he knows what I am. . . ." Dana murmured.

"I would say that he has always known."

"Fenris said that was why he brought me to the Tower. But to do what, exactly?"

"I don't know."

"And Aonia? What does she want of me?"

"I don't know that either. Aonia isn't here; she speaks to you from my world, and from the day I crossed the threshold to be with you, I have not been in contact with other spirits. I believe Aonia must have unfinished business in the world of the living, and that is why she is trying to communicate with you."

"And the old blind woman in the town?"

"She was simply a spirit who was too used to living there to be able to cross over."

Dana said nothing. Her head was buzzing with questions, but the most urgent one she didn't dare ask aloud.

"I made a mistake," said Kai, reading her thoughts. "I was not supposed to become involved, but . . . I have grown too fond of you, Dana. I shouldn't have let that happen."

Dana closed her eyes. Kai had placed special emphasis on the words "too fond." "And now what is going to happen to us?" she asked.

Kai did not answer immediately, and Dana knew that was a bad sign.

"I think I would have fallen in love with you even if you weren't the one person in the world who can hear me," he finally whispered. "So I have thought a lot about us, about how neither of us is to blame, how it was inevitable." He looked into her eyes. "When my time is up, I will have to return to the Other Side. My powers are fading quickly. Soon I won't even be able to pick things up."

"Your time?"

"I died when I was sixteen," he answered in a hoarse voice. "My life as Kai cannot last much longer."

Dana felt as if she were going to faint. She was already sixteen. How much time did they have left? Days? Weeks? Months? "You told me you would never leave me. Is there nothing we can do?"

"Nothing."

She wanted to put her arms around him, bury her face in his shoulder and cry, but she repressed the impulse. She would have been embracing only air. "Why didn't you tell me this sooner?"

"Why? It was best to enjoy our time together. If you had known that I would have to leave you, you would never have been completely happy. And you must enjoy life to the fullest, Dana. I say that out of experience."

"You said that we'd never . . ." Dana refused to hear what he was saying.

"Never; that part is true. We will be separated for a while when I go. But some day we will meet on the Other Side, and that time it will be forever . . . if you still remember me."

"I will never forget you."

Kai smiled sadly. "That's what you say now. But you are young, and you will meet others. . . ."

Before Dana could answer, a terrible crash shook the lodge, and an enormous hairy shape hurtled through a hole in the barrier of trees.

"Fenris!" Dana cried, jumping to her feet.

"Didn't you say we were safe?" Kai protested.

Dana didn't reply. She quickly reinforced the enchantment and sealed the hole, then immediately chanted a spell to stupefy Fenris, who lay semiconscious on the floor.

"What should we do with him?" asked Kai.

Dana knelt down beside the elfwolf. She connected her aura to that of the beast and tried to calm it. The rational part of Fenris was bravely struggling against his savage side, and his senseless suffering pained her. She tried to communicate encouragement to him, not knowing whether it would reach him.

"It's almost as if he were drugged," Kai commented when Fenris moaned.

"He won't be like this much longer. Enchantments are not miracle changes, you know."

"Then we should just tie him up, or immobilize him somehow."

Dana's eyes lighted on an old wooden table over in a corner. "I can make a cage from that. If I reinforce it with magic, it will do the job. All I have to do is move Fenris over there." She put out a hand toward the elfwolf, and he levitated one foot off the ground, then two. Under Kai's approving gaze, she propelled him toward the corner table. However, she miscalculated his weight and the distance; the magical energy fell short, and the elfwolf dropped to the floor.

Dana cringed and ran to see if the fall had roused the wolf from his stupefaction.

"Wait!" Kai stopped her. "Did you hear that? That hollow sound?"

Dana tapped her foot on the floor around Fenris. "There's something down there," she said.

"It must be a cellar. Maybe we can hide there if the wolves manage to get in."

Dana got down and examined the floor by the light of a magical fire. "A trapdoor," she reported. She tugged at it in vain. Quickly she traced the letters of a charm on the door. It lifted open easily, giving access to the space beneath. Dana peered in, but it was too dark to see. She looked toward Kai, who nodded. She extinguished all the magical fires except one, and directed that one into the cellar. The pale light revealed a set of large, beautiful marble stairs.

Dana quickly levitated Fenris under the table and wove a magical net to hold him there. Then she and Kai roused the horses and started down the stairs, closing the trapdoor behind them.

The stairway opened onto a large, elegant corridor. As they stepped out into the corridor, two rows of magic torches flared up along either side of the passageway. They walked along the corridor for some distance until they saw a majestic door flanked by two slender columns.

It filled Dana with wonder. "It looks like some kind of temple," she whispered. "What do you think it could be?"

"*That* is what we came to find out," said Kai. "What Aonia wanted us to find."

Dana put out her magical flame and walked toward the door, while Kai and the horses followed in silence.

11
Trapped

Fenris lay on the dusty floor in the darkness of the lodge. As long as the full moon exercised its power over him, the elfwolf was concerned only with his imprisonment, which kept him from getting up and chasing after the young, tender girl and her tasty horses. The howls of his pack came to him from outside the magical wall of trees, but he was scarcely conscious of their futile attempts to claw an opening in the tightly woven barrier.

Then, suddenly, it was as if a ray of light sliced through his awareness. First he panted and flexed his hairy paws; then he growled. When the light grew even brighter, and he felt the stirrings of another consciousness, he gave himself over to it.

Soon he opened his eyes and was able to sit up a little. He looked at his paws just as the hair and claws were disappearing, returning to fine, long-fingered elf hands. "I'm beginning to be myself again," he said out loud, and clung to that thought. He could tell that his canine teeth were back to near-normal size, that his snout was shrinking, and that the hair that had covered his face was receding to smooth bronze skin.

The elf stretched like a cat and swept a hand through his coppery hair. Then his eyes opened wide — before him knelt the figure of the Lord of the Tower.

"Is it daylight yet?" was all Fenris could say.

The Maestro shook his head. His gray eyes studied the elf. "Where have they gone?" he asked softly. He dissolved Dana's magical net, and Fenris rolled out from under the table and stumbled to his feet. The transformation had drained him of strength. He was pale and tired; dark circles ringed his eyes. Every bone in his body ached, and it was painful even to breathe. As he leaned against the table for support and looked at the Maestro, he realized they were in the old hunting lodge and decided not to ask what they were doing there. The room was empty except for the Maestro and a small figure standing behind him in the shadows.

"Where have they gone?" the magician asked again.

Fenris was almost too tired to think. Nevertheless, he knew he must try to remember. They had followed the unicorn through the forest. The effects of the circle of purification had not lasted very long, and he had told Dana to get away quickly, and then . . .

He shuddered. That was all he could remember. Had

she managed to escape? Or had he, blinded by the irrational fury of a lycanthrope, a werewolf, caught up with her and . . . ?

"She is alive," the Maestro assured him.

Fenris closed his eyes and concentrated on the sensations he had experienced most recently. He remembered a savage pursuit, like all his adventures under the full moon; he remembered two hard thumps and a sense of peace when she . . .

Dana had come over to him and had used her magic to calm him. Then . . .

He concentrated on the present, and almost involuntarily he looked down at his feet. The Maestro followed the direction of his eyes and saw the trapdoor.

"Good work," the magician said.

The enormous, majestic door opened with a squeal. Dana and Kai stopped, openmouthed, as a wide beam of golden light bathed them from head to foot. It was so bright that they could not see what lay beyond.

Dana drew upon her courage and stepped inside. Kai went with her, surprised that the horses, which had been nervous all evening, now seemed completely calm.

As their eyes became accustomed to the radiance, they found that the source of the light was a huge, tree-shaped, gold statue in the center of the room. In its shade were many sculpted figures — mammals, reptiles, various flowers and plants — and its branches sheltered numbers of gold birds. Its roots reached into a small pool, and fish and amphibians fashioned of gold hid in the water.

"This must be a sacred place," Dana murmured in awe. "Who would they be worshipping here?"

"Mother Earth," Kai answered.

Once Dana was able to tear her eyes away from the golden tree, she saw that this temple-like chamber was really a small natural cave. Silver and gold embellished its rock walls, and the floor was paved with slabs of marble, which dropped away into the pool.

And beside the pool stood the unicorn, his starry eyes focused on Dana and Kai. Had he been watching them from the beginning? Dana felt a thrill at seeing him again. This close and in the golden light, the unicorn was so beautiful it seemed to make her heart turn over.

"Go over to him," Kai said. "I think he's waiting for you."

She walked forward hesitantly. The unicorn waited till she reached the edge of the pool, then dipped his head gracefully and brushed the surface of the water with his magic horn. Then he lifted his head and looked at her — and all at once disappeared.

Dana choked back a moan and reached out to where the gorgeous creature had just stood. She heard Kai's voice at her side.

"What is in the pool, Dana?"

She leaned over the water. "It doesn't seem very deep. I can see something glistening on the bottom."

"Could that be the unicorn's treasure?"

Dana's heart beat faster. "I think he was showing it to *us*!" she exclaimed. "Do you realize that?"

"I realize it," a soft voice said behind them. "And now you two have shown it to me."

Kai and Dana turned. Standing at the door were the Maestro, Maritta, and Fenris.

"You risked your life again, despite my warnings, Dana," said the magician, walking toward her. "And not only have you survived, you have come farther than anyone before you. Well done, my pupil. You are the most promising apprentice I have ever had."

Dana blushed at her tutor's compliments, though she did not understand his role in all this.

"You may not be entirely aware of what you have found," the Maestro went on. "Have you heard of the Pool of Reflections? No? Well, then, let me tell you about it. An ancient legend says that these pools exist wherever unicorns are found. On the bottom of each pool lies a small crystal figure of great power, though it is extremely difficult to control and reserved for great sorcerers only — indeed, the magician who possesses it instantly becomes an Archmago. It is an incredible gift."

Dana closed her eyes, sensing where the Maestro was going. "But the unicorn led *me* here," she protested.

The aged magician smiled. "It did indeed. You may collect your prize."

She hesitated a moment, then knelt by the pool and

plunged her hand into the water, trying to touch the sparkling crystal she could see below the surface. Her fingers scraped the marble bottom, but that was all they touched. She watched in amazement as her hand passed through the crystal image as if it didn't exist.

"It seems to be an illusion," she said.

"Exactly." The Maestro was beside her, his voice so unexpectedly near that it startled her. "You can stay here for a decade trying to retrieve it, but you will not succeed. Unicorns guard their secrets well."

"So . . . ?"

"There is an ancient ritual to claim it," the Maestro explained. "If you had waited to search for the pool until you had finished your training, perhaps you might have prevailed. But at this stage you are not ready — the ritual exceeds your ability. So I am afraid I will have to take possession of it in your place."

Dana felt as if she were going to choke with rage at the unfairness of his words. The crystal should be hers!

"He did this on purpose," Kai whispered to her. "The unicorn had never shown itself to him, but he had Fenris to save him from the wolves, and he had you to lead him here. When you didn't succeed the first time, he sent the elf with you to be sure that you could go where he wanted."

Dana's face showed her surprise. Something like that had played on the edges of her mind for a while now, but she had not been able to express it so clearly, perhaps because it hurt her feelings to admit that Fenris had betrayed her. The elf must have been telepathically linked with the Maestro; how else could he have known where they were? He couldn't have followed them into the forest. . . . *They just used me*, she thought.

"I am going to begin the ritual," the Maestro said. "I think that you and Fenris should take the horses out of here."

Dana hated to leave him with the unicorn's treasure, but how could she disobey? She remembered the first rule again: *Never, not for any reason, should an apprentice disobey the Maestro.*

Dana looked for Fenris and saw that he was already leading Alide toward the door.

"Go with him," the Maestro ordered.

Dana exchanged glances with Kai; he too looked worried. She was still considering some way to object when she felt an overwhelming need to follow Fenris. Before she knew what she was doing, she had picked up Moonstar's reins and was heading toward the threshold of the temple.

Dana came to her senses in the corridor, focusing on Kai's face and wondering how she had arrived there.

"Blasted mentalist!" he said. "You've done exactly what he wanted you to do."

"But why — ?" She stopped as darkness filled the corridor, or worse than darkness: She couldn't see or hear or touch anything. She didn't even feel a floor beneath her feet, though she wasn't falling. It was as if she were suspended in air. She moaned and put out a hand, trying to feel something, anything.

"Dana?"

She held her breath. "Fenris? You're here?"

"Me too," Kai said quickly. "The three of us are trapped."

Dana heard Fenris whisper three magical words, followed by a sputtering sound. A small flame burst into life. Its wavering light bathed the faces of the three companions.

"Where are we?" Dana asked.

"In a hole," Fenris said.

"Yes, I can see that. But where?"

"It's a hole without a place. A place without space. A magical prison."

Dana's spirits sank. She had heard about such bewitchments. They were very advanced, and she knew no way to neutralize them.

"You can walk through all eternity and get nowhere," the elf told her. "For that reason, it's best if we stay where we are."

Dana nodded somberly. She believed what he said about the hole, but something else made her angry. "And what are you doing here?" she asked him accusingly.

"What do you mean, what am I doing here? I'm here with you. We defied him, remember? We left the Tower to look for the unicorn on our own."

"Right," Dana groaned. "And he knew from the

beginning. He got exactly what he wanted. We led him to the unicorn."

Fenris's almond-shaped eyes opened wide in surprise. "I should have suspected," he said, his voice disheartened.

"Liar," Dana burst out. "You knew! The Maestro couldn't have got through the woods on his own, and he couldn't have teletransported himself to the cabin without a point of reference. You were his spy!"

Fenris considered her silently. "He used you. Don't think that makes you special. He's used me for fifty years."

Kai grumbled something, but Dana had heard a defeated note in Fenris's voice. "Let him tell his story, Kai," she said. "Maybe we'll learn something."

Fenris took a step back.

"Perhaps you . . ." he began, but corrected himself when he remembered that Dana wasn't alone. "Perhaps the two of you have heard about the land of the elves. It's very far away to the east, across the water. It is a land of beautiful forests and gentle hills, where everything is in harmony and nature is worshipped and respected.

"I was born there, nearly two hundred years ago. So I am a young elf by the standards of my people. But I was never an ordinary elf.

"Very few humans are born with the curse of lycanthropy, or wolf change. Among elves, that syndrome is even rarer, and that is why, when I began to suffer metamorphoses on the nights of the full moon, I knew that my time among my own was ended. My behavior, my presence, my mere existence, threatened the peace of my community.

"No one had compassion for me. They drove me from my home and forced me to wander through the world — either as a rational being or as a beast when the full moon claimed me. I searched everywhere for a cure for my malady, but no one could liberate me from my curse, or at least grant me a little spiritual peace . . . until I met the Maestro.

"At that time he was a young man, but he knew about magic, and he offered to teach me the art of sorcery. More than that, he would take me to a magical place whose power would protect me from my transformations. In exchange . . ."

"In exchange, you had to keep the wolves at bay," Dana finished for him. "That was how he took possession of the Tower. Can he truly control your changes?"

"In the Tower, yes. I protect the Tower, and the Tower protects me. And thanks to the Tower's magic, the Maestro can sometimes protect me when I go out for a brief period of time . . . or reverse the process if I am transformed. But he can also invoke a metamorphosis if it suits him."

"He controls your whole existence," Dana said softly.

"The Tower is my refuge, but it is also my prison. When I came there I was much younger, and I was eager to be free. I kept expecting him to provide me with a true cure. It never occurred to me that the Maestro could bind me to him forever with only a temporary solution. But he knew that I would never have the courage to escape from the Tower and live with my savage side unaided."

"But you did it," Dana observed.

Fenris's eyes were shining as he looked at her. "You are a *Kin-Shannay*. You have been in contact with a deceased Archmaga. The unicorn wanted to give you its treasure. You are destined to do great things, Dana. Maybe at your side I can learn how to free myself from this curse that keeps me a prisoner in my own body." His words had dropped to a barely audible whisper. Dana regarded him with sympathy. His skin was ashen and his breathing ragged; he seemed exhausted. Still, she wasn't sure she could trust him.

"You brought the Maestro here," she reminded him. "You showed him where we were."

Fenris's smile was bitter. "Do you know anyone who has been able to hide anything from the Maestro? I am not sure how I came here — my mind is never very clear when I come out of a transformation — but I imagine that he did whatever he wanted with me . . . as usual. It's obvious that the Maestro wanted you to lead him to the unicorn. And I suspect that's why, the only reason why, he brought you to the Tower six years ago."

"He must have erased my memory after my first try so I wouldn't remember that you could help me," Dana said.

"Because he realized you weren't ready yet." Fenris

spoke as if he were beginning to understand. "The Maestro didn't want to take any chances with you. He is a meticulous and patient man — which is why he is out there and we are in here." The elf sighed. "What I don't understand is what the Archmaga of your visions has to do with all this."

Dana told him what she knew about the identity of the lady in the golden tunic.

"Aonia." The elf thought for a moment. "I don't know that name. So if she is connected to the Tower, she must have died a long time ago and is communicating with you because she wants you, and only you, to have the unicorn's treasure. But why?"

"I don't know. What is it exactly that lies on the bottom of the pool, Fenris?"

"I'm not sure. You heard what the Maestro said. I know of only one book that describes a Pool of Reflections. It says that at the bottom lies a crystal figure in which the unicorn guards its soul. Whoever possesses it may use the unicorn's power forever. Yet that doesn't sound like the full story to me. Besides, no other histories or legends that I've read ever mention the Pool of Reflections or the Soul of Crystal. Very few magicians and scholars take the claims of that book seriously; it has always been considered a fable."

"Well, it would seem that it's more than a fable," Dana replied. "But why would the Maestro . . ."

". . . want to have the unicorn under his control? Use your head, Dana. Any magician would be twice as powerful with a unicorn's horn in his hands."

Dana envisioned the unicorn dead and its horn in the clutches of the Maestro. "He can't do that!" she cried. "The unicorn is sacred!"

"Different people have different views."

"I don't understand. Why would the unicorn lead us to the place where he keeps his soul?"

"Supernatural creatures have their own reasons for doing what they do. No one can understand them."

Dana was trembling with anger and frustration. "We have to do something," she said. "What is the ritual the Maestro is performing?"

"I haven't studied the subject exhaustively, but probably it is the incantation in the book I described. The book claims that the ritual is the only way to capture the unicorn's soul. I seem to remember it required a living sacrifice. . . ." His voice trailed off.

In horror, Dana realized one more piece of the puzzle. "Maritta! He tricked her into coming with him. She's the sacrifice! We have to get out of here and warn her!"

"I can get out of here," Kai said unexpectedly.

"What did you say?"

"I said that I can escape from here, because I am not bound by the laws of your physical world."

"And why didn't you tell us that before now?"

"You wanted to hear his full story! Besides, even if I got out, I couldn't do anything to warn Maritta or free you. So my place is still here by your side."

"What is your friend saying?" asked Fenris.

Dana explained, and the elf frowned in concentration. "If Maritta comes here, we could communicate with her and tell her what is happening."

"Kai is a spirit," Dana said. "Sometimes he can focus his energy enough to move things. If he could guide Maritta in this direction . . ."

"She would be frightened out of her mind and warn the Maestro," Kai objected. "That is, assuming she is still alive."

"You're right," Dana murmured, but she had an idea. She unclasped the amulet she wore around her neck. "Take this to her," she said to Kai. "She will know what it means."

Kai held out his hand. The amulet fell through his ghostly fingers and bobbed in empty air. Dana had not foreseen that, but at least the gleam of the charm allowed her to catch it before it floated away into the darkness.

"What's the matter? Why didn't you take it? I know you can. I've seen you pick up things and move them."

"My forces are fading," Kai said quietly, "the closer it gets to the hour of my leaving."

Dana's heart sank, but her eyes never left his. "Please, try again," she begged. "For your sake and for mine.

Because, as you say, we have very little time left, and I don't want to spend it here in the middle of nowhere."

Kai closed his eyes, and seemingly with all his strength, he folded his fingers around the chain.

"Excellent!" said Fenris when he saw the charm moving past his eyes.

Kai turned to Dana. "I will be back for you," he promised, and softly kissed her forehead.

Maritta stood beside the door to the temple, glancing nervously behind her. Why hadn't Dana and the elf returned? She would have asked the Maestro, but he had told her not to bother him; if the ritual were interrupted, he said, the magic would get out of hand and terrible things would happen.

Now the magus was sitting at the edge of the pool with his legs crossed and his eyes closed. He was chanting something incomprehensible, from time to time tossing golden powders into the air, which cascaded down in colorful mists. Since it was clear that he would be no help to her, Maritta decided to go look for Dana herself.

To her horror she discovered that she could not move her legs. She tried to cry out, but found she could not make a sound, either.

Most other dwarves would have been terrified to learn that they had been bewitched, but Maritta was used to the many faces of magic. She supposed that the Maestro had cast a spell over her to keep her from moving or talking, probably because he didn't think that she could be quiet long enough for him to finish his ritual.

But if that was all there was to it, Maritta wondered, why wasn't Dana back by now?

Suddenly she felt something hard and cold in her hand, and nearly fainted from surprise. When she recovered herself enough to look at the object, she saw that she was holding a metal amulet, a crescent moon with a six-pointed star in the hollow of its curve.

Dana's charm.

Maritta's skin prickled. She didn't know how the pendant had appeared in her hand, but she had no doubt that her friend was trying to contact her. Then something began pushing her. Involuntarily, she opened her mouth to scream, but no sound came out. It was a stroke of good fortune that the Maestro had silenced her, she thought wryly, since she didn't want him to know what was happening.

The something kept nudging her, and her arms windmilled as she fought to keep her balance, but gradually she realized that that something was pushing her persistently toward the door. Toward Dana! Given the sign of the amulet, it could be only Dana's work.

"My little girl needs me!" she told herself, and a terrible fury gripped her. She had lost her Lady of the Tower years ago; she did not want to lose Dana too. That old goat of a magus had gone too far. She gritted her teeth and struggled to get free. With a supreme effort, she lifted one foot and then the other.

She had broken the spell.

Hoping that the Maestro was too deep in his chanting to see what she was doing, Maritta hurried toward the door. Her boots squeaked on the marble floor, but the Maestro failed to notice. She ran down the corridor and never looked back. At the end she could see Alide and Moonstar circling nervously near the marble stairway, but she saw no sign of Dana or Fenris.

The same mysterious force that had been pushing her now abruptly stopped her.

"All right, may I ask what it is you want?" the dwarf grumbled.

The force pushed her this way and that. Then she no longer felt it. She didn't see it or hear it, and somehow she knew it had gone.

Moments later she heard Dana's voice deep inside her mind, quavering but unmistakable: "Maritta?"

12
Aonia's Return

Dana waited a few seconds, holding her breath. Almost immediately the exasperated voice of the dwarf echoed through every corner of their magical prison.

"What is this, girl? What devilish arts are you practicing on me?"

Dana looked at Fenris, overjoyed, and then at Kai, who was back at her side.

"If you move a fraction of an inch from where you are, we will lose contact," Dana warned Maritta. "You are in the same place we are, locked in a kind of fold, or hole, in space. The Maestro has banished us here."

"He's still busy casting his spells," Maritta assured them. "He won't have known that I left."

"Tell her what's happened," Kai prompted Dana.

Telepathically, Dana told Maritta all that had happened that night — following the unicorn, discovering the lodge, Fenris crashing through the barrier of trees in wolf form, and the Maestro finding them in the mysterious sacred temple. When she finished, she was surprised, and a little troubled, by the whirlwind of memories she sensed roaring through Maritta's mind.

"What is it?" she asked.

"Aonia trusted him . . . and he betrayed her," Maritta murmured. "That's why she's come back, to get her revenge."

Dana, Fenris, and Kai exchanged glances.

"Tell us what you know," Dana said slowly.

"He came to the Tower in the midst of a snowstorm." The dwarf spoke in a low voice, as if she were afraid the Maestro could hear her. "He was a pale, thin, sickly boy, and Aonia took him in, because in the Tower everyone was welcome. She raised him as if he was her son, and she taught him the art of sorcery.

"I always knew, though, that he didn't love her in return. He didn't love anyone except himself.

"I was just the cook in the Tower, but Aonia trusted me, and she often came down to visit with me. She appreciated my good sense, she used to say. She would tell me how the boy was growing up, and how proud she was of him. But when he reached adolescence, she began to see how ambitious he was and the problems that might cause.

She attributed it to the rebellious spirit so common at that age. Poor Aonia!"

Maritta sighed. None of the prisoners dared say a word.

"There were many rumors about the Lady of the Tower," Maritta continued. "One of them, one of many, said that she had been touched by the unicorn and wielded its power. There may have been some truth in that rumor; anyhow, the boy believed it.

"I'm not really sure how it happened. I don't know how that pale, skinny child could have turned against Aonia, or how he overcame her. Maybe she didn't expect his betrayal, or maybe she couldn't face the full extent of his ambition in a person she loved.

"And so we lost the Lady of the Tower at the hands of her ungrateful adopted son. It was a death the Valley lamented for a very long time. But it had other, far-reaching consequences. . . ."

"The curse . . ." Dana whispered.

"The boy had forgotten the primary rule of sorcery: An apprentice must never rebel against his teacher, because if he does, and his mentor curses him, the curse will follow him through eternity."

Fenris paled. He looked at Dana, who understood what he was thinking: Rebelling was precisely what they were doing now.

"Aonia died, but before she did, she put a curse on her apprentice and on every creature who dared come to live in the Tower: The wolves would not rest until they avenged her murder. Then you couldn't go out day or night without fearing those magical beasts — they were so bloodthirsty they'd rip apart anything they could get their teeth on." Maritta was silent for a moment. "In the end, all the inhabitants of the Tower fled, and only he and I were left.

"I was hiding in the kitchen when the wolves poured in to tear the young man to pieces. I heard him fight back, though, as he searched the Lady's chambers. He thought Aonia kept the unicorn's horn in her rooms, and once he found it, the power would be his.

"When he discovered that Aonia had made sure he could not find what he was looking for, his screams echoed all over the valley. I was still hiding beneath the sink, and I thought the wolves had killed him and the Lady's curse had been fulfilled.

"The wolves left the Tower without catching my scent. But after that, they roamed the forest day and night, and never let travelers pass anywhere near the Tower. When I saw that, it made me think that the apprentice had escaped after all, and Aonia's soul was still clamoring for revenge.

"And so the years went by. The spell hung over the Tower, and I survived thanks to the enchanted kitchen pantry. I never ventured outside, where I knew the wolves were always waiting.

"Until one evening when that accursed man came back along the road through the valley. He had someone with him, and, mysteriously, the wolves gave way to them. He opened the magic gate, rode up to the Tower, and climbed to the highest floor to take possession of the chambers that had once belonged to the Golden Lady. After that, we could go out in the valley during the day again; he was able to accomplish that much. He also claimed for himself the title of Maestro and Lord of the Tower. He never paid much attention to me, but I always knew that he'd come back to look for the thing that he had failed to find and that must have become his obsession: the secret of the unicorn's power, the secret that made him betray Aonia.

"*And* I also knew that someday she would come back to avenge herself."

Maritta seemed to have finished. Dana gave Fenris a piercing look.

"I swear I didn't know about any of that," he said.

His voice sounded in Maritta's mind, and she returned to the present. "Is that elf with you, girl? Do you think you can trust him?"

Dana regarded Fenris. She wasn't sure. But as another part of her mind reviewed Maritta's story, she realized why the Maestro had brought her to the Tower. He knew that Aonia would be able to reveal the location of the Soul of Crystal only to a *Kin-Shannay*. And once Aonia communicated with her, all he would have to do was follow Dana and claim the precious treasure for his own. But if that was so obvious, why had Aonia insisted so strongly on Dana's looking for it?

"Open the door."

Dana jumped. The voice of the dead sorceress had sounded in her mind, clear as a bell.

"What is it?" Fenris asked.

Dana frowned. Perhaps her imagination had played a trick on her. But the voice spoke again: "Open the door."

"Door? What door?" she said to the voice.

"What is Kai telling you?" Fenris asked.

Dana shook her head. "It isn't Kai. It's Aonia."

"The lady is talking to you now!" Maritta whispered. "Then it's true!"

"She asked me to open the door," Dana told her. "I'm afraid I don't know what that means."

"She wants to come back to the world of the living," Maritta said. "To destroy that wicked man once and for all."

"But where *is* the door? What must I do?"

"Haven't you understood yet?" Kai's voice was intense. "Dana, *you* are the door."

Dana stepped back, her eyes wide with fright.

"*Kin-Shannay*," the elf guessed. "The portal."

"Stop! That's enough!" Dana shrieked. "Stop talking like that! What do you want of me?"

Kai put his arms around her, and his unearthly touch calmed her as always. She closed her eyes and tried to breathe normally.

"Project your mind toward another dimension," he said softly. "Look for the place I come from. Look for Aonia. She will be waiting for you."

"And where is that dimension? Where must I search?"

"Within yourself. Each of us carries both life and death within us," Kai whispered. "Your world and mine are not in opposition, they are parallel and complementary. And *you* can breach the slender gap that separates them. You are a door between the two planes."

"But . . ."

"Close your eyes and listen to Aonia's voice. Give yourself over to it. She wants to come back, and we don't want to deprive her of that satisfaction, do we?"

Kai smiled, and Dana smiled in return. Of course she could connect the world of the living and the world of the dead; after all, she had always had him. . . . She closed her eyes.

"Dana," said Aonia's voice. "*Kin-Shannay*. Open the door."

Dana settled her awareness on the voice and cleared her mind of everything else. She willed herself to pay attention only to the voice, to let it come to her more and more strongly.

"*Kin-Shannay*. Open the door."

She went to meet the voice that was calling her with

such urgency. Her mind sank to the depths of her soul, and she walked on the border between life and death.

"Open the door . . .

"Bring the legitimate Lady of the Tower back to her home. . . .

"The door . . ."

Back home.

Dana's pallor deepened; she gulped as if she were going underwater, and her hands flailed in the air. Just as her fingers closed around a warm, real, physical hand, she lost consciousness, and a pair of arms embraced her firmly.

Dana's heart and breath stopped. Her body was still somewhere between life and death, but her mind had already crossed over.

She found herself face-to-face with Aonia, the Lady of the Tower. Seen in her full glory, she was even more beautiful and magnificent than her own shimmering vision. Dana knew that if this sorcerer succeeded in returning to avenge his crime, the Maestro was in serious trouble.

Aonia smiled. "Thank you for coming to free me from the Other Side."

Dana heard the voice in her heart, not in her ears. "I am honored to be of service," she said, smiling back.

"Let me go home," Aonia said.

The apprentice held out her hand. "Whenever you wish, ma'am."

The Lady's pale hand pressed hers. She was mortally

cold, reminding Dana that the woman was a spirit. Everything began to whirl as the two of them, hand in hand, began the dizzying journey back to the world of the living.

Dana's back arched and a spasm shook her body as consciousness returned to her abruptly. She raised her head, trying desperately to breathe, fighting a feeling of suffocation. She trembled with fear and cold until she sensed a pair of strong arms holding her reassuringly.

"Kai!" she said, smiling.

"Kai? I'm afraid not," replied a soft, melodious voice.

Dana blinked and saw that she was in Fenris's arms. Her gaze found Kai standing a little apart, watching with a forlorn expression.

Dana got to her feet and looked around.

"Are you all right?" asked Kai.

"Where is Aonia? She was with me!"

Fenris looked perplexed.

"It's still only the three of us," Kai observed.

Just then, a brilliant light sliced through the dark of the magical hole, and the next thing they knew, all three were standing bewildered on the marble floor of the corridor. Moonstar saw her mistress and trotted over to nuzzle her.

"What . . ." murmured Dana.

Aonia was gone, but Maritta stood among them with her feet planted firmly and hands on her hips.

"Well, it's time for a little fun," said the dwarf with a

strange smile. She turned and marched down the corridor toward the entrance to the temple.

"She's mad!" said Fenris. "We should get out of here while we can!"

Dana was about to stop Maritta, but Kai's unearthly hand held her back. She saw in his expression a mixture of jubilation, comprehension, and curiosity. His eyes never left the dwarf, who had reached the doorway to the hall of Mother Earth.

"Come on!" he said, and started running after Maritta.

"Wha . . . ?" said Fenris. "Where are you going?"

Dana couldn't answer as she followed Kai. The elf magician hesitated only a moment, then ran after her.

Maritta had slipped inside the hall and was standing in the very spot she had abandoned to come to Dana's aid. The Maestro had just finished the first portion of the ritual. He turned toward her.

"You are still here, my dear?"

Maritta gave him an enchanting smile.

The Maestro frowned slightly and tried to burrow into her mind. An impenetrable barrier stopped him. "I must be tired," he muttered. "But it's nothing important." With a sweep of his hand he nullified the spell he had cast on her, unaware that it had been neutralized some time before.

"Come closer," he said.

Maritta obeyed.

The Maestro rubbed his eyes. He was tired, yes, but he also knew that he had to perform the sacrifice if he wanted to receive the Soul of Crystal. At first he had thought of Dana, but the unicorn seemed to respect her, and to sacrifice her might be counterproductive. As for the elf, he could still be useful. That left the old dwarf.

The ceremonial dagger, its hilt set with precious stones, lay on the floor. He picked it up and reached out to seize his victim. But before he could touch her, she said, "Suren, you have fallen very low. I would never have imagined that you would forget everything I taught you so quickly."

The Maestro stiffened. It had been more than half a century since anyone called him by that name, a cursed name that he was sure had died with the person who had given it to him.

He looked at Maritta. The dwarf's bright eyes were filled with determination.

"Have you forgotten me?" she continued in a clear, soft voice not at all the dwarf's own. "I taught you magic and raised you like a son. You had no home or family, and I gave you both. And not only did you turn against me, you usurped the Tower and its treasures, and now you've come looking for something your miserable heart doesn't deserve."

"Aonia!" The sorcerer's lips spat out the name.

The dwarf smiled bitterly. "You are surprised to find me here? You knew who and what your student was, and you hoped her powers would tempt me to show her the way to the temple. You hoped that I would choose her to receive the power of the unicorn. But you thought she was too inexperienced to succeed, didn't you? You underestimated your disciple, Suren. You thought that she would not be able to bring me back."

The sorcerer shouted something unintelligible and lifted his dagger to plunge it into this annoying dwarf who was tormenting him with voices from the past. Quick as lightning, however, she raised her arms and uttered an enchantment. The Maestro staggered back and his body thudded against the wall of the cave.

"You defeated me once, but you will not do it again," Maritta announced. "I have learned that there is no room for compassion when dealing with you."

Fenris and Dana watched from the doorway, astonished.

"Aonia is back," Kai explained with a smile, confirming Dana's own thought. "You allowed her spirit to pass into this world; then all she needed was a body in which to confront the traitor . . . and she found Maritta."

Maritta walked inexorably toward the aged Maestro, who lay crumpled against the wall. "My curse has been pursuing you for a long time, Suren," she said. "You sealed your fate the day you sent me to the world of the dead."

With that, four enormous gray wolves materialized behind Maritta. Dana gasped and moved closer to Fenris.

But the wolves' eyes were fixed only on the Lord of the Tower, their slavering tongues protruding from teeth sharp as daggers.

The Maestro moaned in fear and began muttering a spell.

"The wolves know that Fenris is not the only one in the Tower who stays awake at night," said Maritta. "They know their howls fill your worst nightmares, that you hear them even when you're awake. You have always known what your end would be."

The Maestro spoke the last words of his enchantment and raised his hands over his head. Blue sparks burst from his fingertips . . . then instantly dissipated. He stared at his hands. The wolves began their low growling.

"You no longer have any power over me," Maritta assured him. "Your magic doesn't work because your time has come. The spirits of the dead are calling for vengeance."

The sorcerer dropped to his knees and buried his head in his hands. Dana held her breath; she knew the extent of the Maestro's power and was dumbfounded to see him this way, as defenseless as a child.

Now Maritta's gaze shifted. She regarded him with curiosity. "Come over here," she ordered. "Peer into the pool and tell me what you see."

The magician looked at her with suspicion, but the wolves slunk away and let him pass.

"Kneel and look into the pool," Maritta said again.

Reluctantly, the Maestro obeyed. He walked to the pool, knelt beside it, and looked in.

"I see the Soul of Crystal," he said after a bit.

"You see only what you want to see. Look closer."

The Maestro bent over the pool again.

Several long moments passed, then the aged magician screamed with terror and fell back, covering his eyes. Dana felt an icy blast sweep the room. The once powerful Lord of the Tower was lying on the floor, knees drawn up to his chin, sobbing. His slight shoulders shook as if a glacial cold had penetrated his bones.

Maritta bent over him. "Do you know what it was you saw?" she asked. Then she whispered something into his ear. The Maestro looked up with an expression of absolute horror, and Maritta straightened with satisfaction.

"Now you understand what the unicorn's treasure is, and why you were destined not to have it," she told him.

As the dwarf was speaking, Dana noticed a change in the Maestro's face. "Maritta!" she screamed, but it was too late. With a howl of rage, the sorcerer sprang up and in one explosive burst of power swept away everything around him. Maritta was thrown back, and Fenris and Dana shielded themselves behind the columns of the temple door. When Dana looked again, the wolves had disappeared, Maritta lay sprawled on the floor, and the Maestro, reinvigorated, was standing in the middle of the sacred chamber.

"You want to play, do you, Aonia?" He laughed. To

Dana, he seemed possessed. "All right, then, we'll play. You say that I underestimated Dana. You are right, dear lady. But you underestimated me once in the past, and now you have done so again. You've been on the Other Side without your magic for many years now, while I am no longer the clumsy apprentice you knew. I will offer you a challenge, Aonia. But it will not take place here. We will play this out in my realm."

He looked toward the entranceway where Dana and Fenris were hiding. Dana felt her knees weaken with the thought of what might come.

"No!" yelled Fenris.

"Yes," said the Maestro. "Yes, my good apprentice."

A flash of light forced Dana to close her eyes.

When she opened them, everything was quiet. She saw Kai leaning against the wall and Maritta getting up from the floor, but there was no trace of the wolves or Fenris or the Maestro.

"He was right," Maritta said quietly. "I underestimated him. Desperation has given him strength, and now he has the advantage."

"He has the advantage? Where is he?" Dana asked.

"Can't you guess? He's gone back to the Tower."

"And that's why he took Fenris." Dana understood now. "But what happened, exactly?"

"You truly want to know?" said Maritta, staring hard at Dana. "Come over here. Look into the pool and tell me what you see."

Dana frowned, unable to understand why her friend was treating her the way she had treated the Maestro.

"Didn't you hear me?" Maritta insisted.

When Dana didn't move, Maritta was before her in two strides. She raised her hands, and for a moment her eyes glittered. Dana fell to her knees.

"Do not defy me, girl," she said dangerously. "Obey."

Dana felt faint, but at the same time, against her will, her body began to crawl toward the pool.

"No!" yelled Kai, running to help her.

Maritta waved her hand and he stopped as if he had hit a wall. "Dana!" he screamed, beating his hands against the magic barrier that kept him from reaching her.

Maritta did not relent. Dana knelt over the pool. She didn't want to look — she had seen what happened to the Maestro — but Aonia's magic forced her to open her eyes.

"Tell me what you see," Maritta said.

Dana looked down and concentrated on the brilliance at the bottom of the pool. She couldn't make out anything in particular at first, but she drew on her courage and kept staring. Soon the water moved in gentle waves and an image began to take shape beneath the surface. She wanted to look away — surely she would see some monster or demon. But as the form became clearer, to her amazement, she saw the image of the unicorn moving toward her. Just as he was about to reach her, his image faded into a brilliant aureole gleaming with all the colors of the rainbow. It was so beautiful it brought tears to Dana's eyes. She felt an indescribable sense of peace and well-being, and smiled as the light came toward her and enveloped her.

Then a hand softly touched her shoulder and pulled her away from the pool. Dana turned reluctantly and met Maritta's eyes, which were filled with affection, happiness, and hope.

"What was it I saw in the well?" Dana dared ask.

Maritta's lips turned up in a smile. "Your soul," she said.

Dana was still kneeling on the floor, dazed. Kai knelt beside her and wrapped his arms around her shoulders. "You taught her well," Aonia's spirit told Kai, who gave her a long, steady look in return. "Congratulations. She would not be the person she is now without your influence."

"But what happened?" whispered Dana. "Isn't that the Soul of Crystal at the bottom of the pool?"

"Your Maestro misinterpreted the words of his book," said Maritta. "There is nothing on the bottom. The pool of the unicorn reflects the soul of the person looking into it. What the Lord of the Tower saw was terrible for him, and it has completely unbalanced him. But you . . ."

"I saw marvelous things," murmured Dana.

"Yes, that is good." Maritta nodded. "And because of that, when you become a full sorcerer, the unicorn will touch you with his horn and bestow his power upon you. That is the secret of the unicorn's horn, and the secret of his power. We have all learned something today. I learned that I cannot vanquish him on my own. I will still need your help, Dana."

"*My* help?" Dana repeated. "I am only an apprentice."

"You will be much more than that when the unicorn gives you its power."

Dana shook her head and was quiet for a moment. "I don't understand," she said at last. "And I don't want to kill the Maestro. But I do want to rescue Fenris. I owe it to him. For that reason, and that reason only, I will go with you to the Tower and do battle against the Maestro."

"I expected no less," said Maritta with a nod of approval.

She made a pass with her hand, the three of them disappeared, and once again the temple of Mother Earth was cloaked in silence.

13
The Test of Fire

Up in the top of the Tower, the Maestro was working feverishly. His enormous study was in great disorder. Magical objects, herbs, and protective amulets were strewn across his shelves, and stacks of leather-bound volumes teetered in a precarious pile on his desk. Fire crackled in the fireplace, sending shadows across the room, and a small incense burner in the corner threw out constantly changing swirls of multicolored smoke.

The Lord of the Tower stood before his desk, poring over a manuscript. From time to time an arcane word or two escaped his lips. At the back of the room, the night air blew through a large open window, where Fenris stood with his back to the study. Heavy snow was falling, but the elf seemed not to care. He could see a horde of yellow eyes down in the forest, all of them focused on the top of the Tower, but as long as he was there, they would not dare come any closer. *Maybe I should just let them in,* he thought bitterly. *At least that way I would be doing something useful.*

The Maestro whirled around, and the elf magician realized that the sorcerer had effortlessly picked up his thoughts.

"Dana and Aonia will soon be here," he told the Maestro without turning to look at him.

"Yes," the sorcerer responded, "I am expecting them."

Fenris sighed to himself. For the first time he was realizing how alone he had been all his years in the Tower, and this new sense had led him to hope that Aonia's spirit would be able to defeat the Maestro. But that had not happened in the temple, and overpowering him in the Tower would be much more difficult.

The elf stole a glance at his mentor. The Lord of the Tower was walking nervously around the room, muttering unintelligible words and looking distraught. Fenris didn't know what the aged magician had seen in the Pool of Reflections, but it seemed clear that the vision had dissolved, temporarily at least, his long-held ambition to control the spirit of the unicorn. What would the Maestro do now? It could not be anything good. Perhaps the Lord of the Tower had even gone mad. *But that wouldn't change things much either,* Fenris thought, no longer caring that the magician was probably reading his mind.

Despondent, Fenris returned to his vigil. Snow beat against the ancient walls of the Tower. At its base, he could see, the wolves were still watching, waiting to catch him off guard and rush inside for their revenge. *I should let them in,* Fenris thought again.

"Don't even think it, apprentice," the Maestro warned him, even though Fenris was not an apprentice any longer. "Try it and you will die before the first of those predators puts one foot in the garden."

The elf didn't answer. He had no choice but to resign himself to life as the Maestro's slave. Maestros could live extraordinarily long lives, perhaps as long as the normal life of an elf. And if that were true of the Lord of the Tower, Fenris would have to spend the remaining six hundred years of his life a prisoner in this place with no promise of relief or friendship.

The Maestro chortled at the thought.

Fenris didn't bother to reply.

Dana, Kai, and Maritta materialized in the now empty kitchen. Cold and dark, it bore no resemblance to the welcoming refuge Dana was used to.

"What do we do now?" asked Kai.

"Well, you can be sure that the Maestro knows we're here," said Dana. She turned to Maritta. "Why did you bring us back to the kitchen?" she asked. "Now we have to climb the twelve stories to the top of the Tower. We've lost the element of surprise."

The dwarf did not answer. She was digging through a trunk.

"Here," she said to Dana, when she'd found what she was looking for. "Put this on."

It was a gray hooded cape, at first glance nothing out of the ordinary, but Dana knew it must be something magical.

"It's to make us invisible," Maritta explained, wrapping herself in another just like it. "It will cloak your mind and hide your magical energies from the Maestro. Even if he has observed our arrival in the Tower, he will not be able to tell exactly where we are."

Quickly Dana put the cape on.

"If you know where to look, the Tower is filled with very useful magic props, things the Maestro has never paid much attention to," Maritta said. "But there is still one detail to settle. Kai must stay here."

Kai froze. "I'm going with Dana," he protested. "I'm not going to leave her alone."

"I know that it is your duty," Maritta said soothingly, "and I also know that you're not protecting her out of simple obligation. But the Lord of the Tower can sense your presence. The best way to protect Dana, Kai, is to stay far away from her. At least for now."

Kai understood, but his eyes were filled with worry. "I don't want you to go," he told Dana in a low voice. "It's so dangerous."

"I don't want to leave you, either," she said. "But I'll be back."

Maritta was waiting at the door. Dana reached out to touch Kai's hand, and for a moment his fingers felt as warm and real as her own. Knowing that some part of her would stay with him in the kitchen, Dana joined Maritta. They left without another word and, like shadows, began the climb to the top of the Tower.

The Maestro stopped a moment in the center of the study and frowned. "Where are they?" he growled. "Where have they gone?"

Fenris, still at the window, glanced at him and smiled to himself.

The aged magician spoke the words of a spell and made a pass with his hand, and immediately a miniature image of the Tower appeared before him. He studied it closely, and with another wave of his hand, the image began to turn, allowing him to observe the Tower from all angles.

"They've put on magic cloaks," he guessed. "Very clever. But . . . what's this?" On the lowest floor of the Tower image, a small point of blue light sparkled. "In the kitchen? I can't believe they would stay there so long, eh? It must be a decoy."

He kept watching the point of light, and after a bit a half smile crossed his lips. "Ah," he said. "Why, it's Kai."

And Fenris did not like the tone of his voice.

*   *   *

Dana and Maritta trudged up the enormous spiral stairway. The dwarf was panting with exhaustion.

"When I was a young sorceress and ruled the Tower," she gasped, "I could do this with no difficulty. But Maritta never did like stairs, and after all, I am in her body."

Dana nodded, a little surprised. Sometimes it was difficult to remember that it was Aonia speaking, not Maritta.

"Why don't we teletransport ourselves there?"

"If we cast the slightest spell, our invisibility would no longer hide us from the Maestro," Maritta warned. "Keep that in mind, Dana."

They continued up the stairway, floor after floor. The Tower had never seemed so tall to Dana as it did now.

"Esteemed ladies . . ."

Dana and Maritta stopped. The Maestro's voice echoed off the stone walls and resounded through the stairwell.

"You are out there somewhere," his voice continued. "It really doesn't matter where. I know you can hear me."

The voice paused, and Dana felt the hair on the back of her neck rise.

"I am speaking to you, my dear visitors, to propose a pact. I have in my power someone very dear to one of you, and I know you don't want to see him suffer."

Dana froze.

"Don't worry," said Maritta. "He won't harm the elf. Without him he can't defend himself from the wolves."

"I know what you are thinking," the sorcerer's voice broke in. "Well, for once, I can't *know* that, since you have so kindly hidden your thoughts from me. But I can imagine it perfectly. Allow me to clarify one thing: I am not referring to Fenris. I am talking about someone you left behind in the kitchen."

A scream welled up in Dana's throat, and Maritta had to grab hold of her to keep her from running back downstairs. "It's a bluff," the dwarf told her. "He can't harm Kai; Kai's a spirit."

The Maestro's soft, quiet laugh echoed down the stone corridors. "*Sul'iketh*," was all he said.

Dana did not recognize the word, but Maritta had turned mortally pale. "What is it?" Dana whispered, trembling. "What is *sul'iketh*?"

"An ancient enchantment."

"And what does it do?" asked Dana. When the dwarf did not immediately reply, Dana felt a stab of fear deep inside her.

"It's a spell for trapping ghosts," Maritta finally said. "He can't harm Kai, but he can seal him away for all eternity."

Dana moaned and held her head. She *knew* she should never have left Kai. "I'm sorry," Maritta whispered. "I didn't think he could be in any danger."

Behind the hood, Dana wept. "You know I will do anything," she murmured, "anything he asks, as long as he sets Kai free."

"Yes," said Maritta quietly. "And I'm afraid that's exactly what he knows too."

The Maestro's voice boomed down the stairway.

"You will be wondering what I want in exchange for liberating the spirit. It's very simple. I have chased the secret of the unicorn all my life, and now all my plans have been frustrated. Very well; I can forgo the magic of the unicorn. But there is something in this Tower that is much more powerful than that. I will let the spirit go, *Kin-Shannay*, if for the rest of your life you will work your magic according to my wishes."

The blood rushed from Dana's head, and she collapsed against the wall.

"And to be certain that you do not deceive me," the sorcerer went on, "you will put your whole mind at my disposal. If you do that, I will free Kai. In return, you will be my slave. And of course you will tell Aonia to go back where she came from and never, ever, return to the world of the living."

Dana looked at Maritta beseechingly.

"I don't see any way out," Maritta said slowly. "We could confront him, but we can't force him to free Kai. Only he can do that, because he is the one who captured him."

"Then what . . . ?"

"The decision is yours, Dana. I cannot tell you what you must do."

Dana closed her eyes. A thousand images of Kai passed through her mind — of Kai with her at the grange, in the

Tower, on horseback, in their sanctuary in the woods. She realized that she could never desert her friend and leave him in the Maestro's power.

"I can't leave him here," she said very quietly. "But how do I know that the Maestro will keep his promise after he enslaves my mind? How will I know that he set Kai free?"

"You will know. If you agree to a magical pact with him, he will be obliged to respect it; otherwise, your mind will not bend to his will. If he doesn't free Kai, you will never be his slave. The Maestro understands the rules governing a sorcerer's power."

Dana opened her eyes. "I have to accept," she said to Maritta. "Kai would do the same for me."

Maritta nodded. "Then we've lost," she said.

Dana looked at her. "I'm so very sorry. You know I would have risked my life for you. But I can't risk Kai's. He doesn't deserve that." She reached for the clasp on her cape. "You must leave, flee the Tower. Don't let him trap you too."

Dana's cape dropped to the floor.

The Maestro's shout of triumph filled the Tower. "Very well, my dear student," he said. "You accept my proposal?"

"I accept."

Maritta moaned.

"Go," said Dana. "Go before I fall into his hands, before he discovers you."

Maritta gave her a long last look filled with admiration

and pity, and then made a magic pass with her hand and disappeared. Dana found herself alone on the enormous spiral stairway.

"Very good," said the Maestro. "Go to the examination room, Dana. We will meet there and talk."

Dana's whole body rebelled, but she climbed up the stairs obediently. The examination room was on the tenth floor — though she could not imagine why the Maestro had chosen that place. She arrived minutes later, pushed open the door and went inside.

Stones adorned with arcane signs paved the floor of the large rectangular room, though a circle in the center was bare of decoration. Disturbing drawings of monsters and magical creatures covered the walls. Three huge crystal chandeliers hung from the ceiling; one shed glittering red light, another violet, and the third green. At the back of the room, between two enormous candelabra, stood the Seat of the Examiner, the throne where the Maestro always sat to test his students.

The aged Maestro sat there now. Behind him stood Fenris, who barely glanced at Dana. The elf seemed unaware of what was happening; Dana suspected that he was concentrating on controlling the wolves.

She approached the throne, and her heart shrank when she saw the small green bottle at the Maestro's feet. She knew that Kai's essence must be sealed inside. She could try to get hold of the bottle, but she remembered that only the Maestro could set Kai free.

"So you are here at last," said the Maestro. "Do you know why I have asked you to come to this room?"

"To close our pact," Dana replied, nervously brushing back her short black hair.

"True enough. But there is something more. I have to watch out for my interests, don't I? Controlling an apprentice's mind is not nearly so satisfying as controlling the mind of a true sorcerer. Let us do things right, *Kin-Shannay*. I have summoned you here to administer the Test of Fire."

A chill ran down Dana's spine. Behind the examining chair, Fenris shifted his feet in agitation, and Dana realized that he must not be as unfocused as he at first appeared. He knew she was being trapped, but he was trapped too. Never had Dana felt so alone.

"You told me that I wasn't ready to be examined."

The magus shrugged his shoulders. "That is your misfortune."

"But if I die trying," she objected, "you will never be able to control me as you desire."

"You would be well advised to stay alive, then," the Maestro said. "Because if you fail and die, your beloved Kai will be bottled for eternity. And eternity is a very, very long time, Dana."

Dana wanted to leap upon the sorcerer and claw out his eyes.

"I know you won't do that," said the aged magician, as though chiding a frustrated child. "And you know why."

Dana nodded and tried to still her mind, to think less violent thoughts. "All right," she said. "I am ready."

She took her place in the center of the circle and, as the rules decreed, recited: "I, Dana, fourth-level apprentice of the Academy of High Sorcery in the Tower of the Valley of the Wolves, *voluntarily*" — she spoke the word with a special irony — "present myself to undergo the Test of Fire, in order to be designated a first-level sorcerer."

The Maestro nodded. "Your presentation, dear student, is approved. We wish you luck."

I'm sure you do, Dana thought to herself. She closed her eyes and let her mind go to the Book of Fire; her studies in sorcery seemed very far away after all that had happened that night.

"Let the examination begin," the Maestro ordered, and light flooded the circle on the floor.

Dana caught Fenris's eye and she saw that she had his support. She could still remember the day three years ago when he had presented himself for the dreaded Test of Fire. He had prepared for years, and he had passed it, but he spent two weeks in bed afterward, recovering from serious burns. Dana had never asked him about the Test of Fire because she knew it was something no sorcerer liked to recall.

The colored lights from the three chandeliers dimmed, and the room sank into soft shadow. Dana prepared herself. She felt how tense her muscles were and sent a warm, relaxing energy through them. She had to pass the test. For Kai.

She tried to empty her mind of anxiety, just remaining alert, ready to perform whatever spell was needed; consciously she began gathering magical energy around her. Fenris had told her she was destined for great things, and she let that thought animate her. She checked her position in the circle; now that the exam had begun, she would not be allowed to step outside it.

The room had grown darker. Suddenly she sensed something approaching and turned to see a blinding ball of fire rushing toward her. She extended her arms and shouted the incantation to create a magic barrier around her, but the fiery ball cut right through it. Dana screamed . . .

. . . and instinctively, she teletransported herself a couple of meters to the right. The ball of fire flashed past her like lightning, barely grazing her, and faded into the darkness.

Dana took a deep breath, but her relief was short-lived. The ground beneath her feet suddenly erupted into flames, then changed in a split second, into an inferno. Dana shouted, alarmed, and recited the spell for levitation, to escape the flames. Even so, her tunic was already on fire, and to extinguish it she had to generate a magic downpour. When the rain had reduced the flames to a carpet of ashes, she looked around cautiously, and discovered the fluctuating outlines of a fire demon observing her mockingly. Its face resembled the heart of a bonfire, and its hair, crackling in the darkness, rose like flames.

"Oh, no," thought Dana, dispirited. She hated the fire demons. They were cruel, debauched creatures that took pleasure from setting everything on fire — especially people. Dana gritted her teeth and prepared to confront it. She would defeat it, of course. She had to, for Kai's sake.

But there was something about this last examination she didn't understand. Normally she was called on to demonstrate her proficiency by conjuring the element she was being tested on. In that case, however, she wasn't the one who had generated the fire; it had sprung from the Maestro's magic, and now Dana had to counter it. And that was absurd, because to fight fire she would have to utilize spells for water, air, even earth. And how, doing that, would she show what she had mastered in the Book of Fire?

She remembered the spell for convoking fire demons. She also knew how to undo those spells. She had that down to perfection. The problem was that she had not summoned this genie, and the book had not explained how to dissolve invocations created by other persons. She had no choice but to fight it and try to destroy it.

The demon laughed and raised its hands toward her. Instantly, its fingers vomited flames.

Dana clenched her teeth and said the words of a spell for a barrier of water. . . .

* * *

"She won't make it," Fenris said. As he spoke, he remembered that he had said those very same words a year earlier, but then about a very different situation.

The Maestro also seemed to remember that scene, because he said, "This time you won't be sent to help her."

Fenris didn't answer. He was thinking of Dana with all the extra energy he possessed, and praying to whomever might hear him that his friend would pass the Test of Fire.

"And then what?" he asked himself. Dana would be a sorcerer, but her will would forever serve the Lord of the Tower. Fenris did not even want to contemplate what the Maestro could do using the powers of a *Kin-Shannay.*

He certainly won't stay locked up here in the Tower, the elf thought. He fixed his almond-shaped eyes on the magic aura that allowed him to watch Dana without distracting her from the test.

Neither he nor the Maestro were aware of the invisible form behind them.

After two long hours of battling the fire, Dana felt that she could resist no longer. The test was like trying to tame a wild animal, though the fire was infinitely more dangerous and deadly: Dana had dodged it, restrained it, commanded it to obey her. But the fire had taken many forms: gigantic blazing balls, circles of flame, small demons laughing and taunting her, even a three-headed dragon with eyes that burned blue. The last creature was an incandescent winged horse that tried to trample her beneath its powerful hooves, nearly forcing her outside the circle. At the moment she destroyed it, something had exploded inside her, and for a few instants she had felt infinitely more powerful than her attacker. Then it was all over, and it seemed as if the battle had emptied her of her last energies.

Now she was lying on the stone floor, drained, gasping for breath. Her violet tunic was singed and tattered, her face sweaty and smeared with soot. She barely had the strength to open her eyes. . . .

Dana glimpsed a faint glow in the darkness above her and her heart pounded. It couldn't be another test. She was not strong enough to stand or to create a circle of protection around herself. What would it be? A phoenix? More fire demons? Another dragon?

She did not have to wait long. The winged horse that Dana thought she had destroyed flew down toward her. She struggled to get to her feet, but her legs would not obey. But she couldn't die now, not now when Kai needed her. The effort to rise brought tears to her eyes, which evaporated instantly in the heat from the descending pegasus.

Dana tried not to think. The winged horse came closer and closer. She shut her eyes.

She felt a gentle warmth on her cheek and heard a soft blowing. When she opened her eyes, an astonishing sight greeted her.

The creature stood beside her, its great head lowered, its soft nose nuzzling her cheek. Its wings were slowly fanning the air. Dana could see the flames radiating from every inch of its hide; she could see its eyes, red as burning coals, its enormous, lethal wings. Yet she was not burning. She was in no pain.

The beast bowed its neck and dropped to its knees beside her.

Could it be that she did not have to destroy the fiery creatures, and instead merely bend them to her will? That after her brutal baptism, fire could no longer harm her? Hesitantly, aware that she had no protection, she reached out to stroke the magical animal's mane. Her fingers passed through the flames, and all she felt was a pleasant warmth on her hand. It was a most strange sensation. Up till that day, she had been able to touch earth, air, and water. And now, after the final test, she could also touch fire. It was beyond her imagining.

With an almost superhuman effort, Dana climbed astride the winged horse's back. It rose to its feet, beat its great wings once or twice, and swung its head around toward its new mistress, as if awaiting instructions.

Dana had passed the Test of Fire.

She felt a savage burst of triumph. "I am a sorcerer," she told herself, and power surged through her and the blazing winged horse. The knowledge afforded her no joy, because she also knew her mind now belonged to the Maestro. But at least, thanks to her, Kai would be free.

"I owed it to you, my dearest friend," she whispered in a hoarse voice. "Now we are at peace."

14

The Farewell

The Maestro nodded, satisfied. He snapped his fingers and the three chandeliers again bathed the examination room in colorful cascades of light. The circle still glowed soft and white, but the fiery winged horse had disappeared. Dana stood there alone, exhausted, singed, yet defiant. The Maestro gave her a small salute. Then he snapped his fingers a second time and her bedraggled violet tunic was transformed into one of magnificent red.

"Well done," he said. "You are now a first-level sorcerer."

Dana raised her chin and looked at him with scorn. "We made a pact. Free Kai, and my will and my magic are yours."

"So be it." The Maestro rose from the Seat of the Examiner and stepped down from the platform to face her. Dana stood her ground. After all she had been through, nothing mattered except Kai's freedom.

Outside, the wolves were still howling. Fenris contemplated the scene with a somber face. Dana thought she could see how sorry he was that he could do nothing to help her.

The Maestro held out his hand. On his palm lay the green bottle that contained Kai's spirit.

"Your freedom for his," he said.

Dana nodded. "Yes, mine for his."

The Maestro raised his hands above her head and began speaking in an arcane tongue. Dana translated the words of the enchantment in her head: "By all the powers of the air and the spirits, I cast this spell, Dana, that you will be bound to me forever in exchange for the freedom of the creature imprisoned by the magic of *sul'iketh*. You will want what I want. You will obey me and respect me as your only lord and master, and you will place your life and your magic at my service for the rest of your life. By the powers of the air and the spirits, I cast this spell upon you, Dana. Your spirit belongs to me, and in return, from this moment on, the creature named Kai is liberated from my power."

Dana felt a glacial cold devouring her soul as the Maestro's consciousness entered her mind and one by one clipped the threads of her will. Her eyes filled with tears, but she struggled to focus on the green bottle in the

Maestro's hands. A thin column of mist rose from it as Dana surrendered to the Lord of the Tower. The last thing she saw through her own eyes was the figure of a blond, green-eyed boy materializing behind the aged magician, looking at her with unparalleled sorrow.

And the last thing Dana said in her own voice was, "Kai-i-i. . . ."

She closed her eyes. When she opened them she would be the slave of the Lord of the Tower. As she heard Kai's voice desperately calling her name, Dana's consciousness plunged into a deep well from which it would never again emerge.

"Dana?"

Dana couldn't see, hear, or feel anything. But in some corner of her mind a voice was speaking her name.

"Dana. Wake up."

Moments went by, during which she was still without sensation. At last she opened her eyes. Her body felt different — light as air. She looked at her hands and discovered she could see right through them.

She tried to scream but could make no sound.

"Dana," said the voice. "Don't be afraid."

Now Dana recognized the voice. It was Aonia's.

She looked around. A panorama of strange, changing colors and vaporous forms played beneath a sunless violet sky. A ghostly fog enveloped everything; but through shreds of mist she could make out the sorcerer, no longer

Maritta but Aonia again, the Archmaga in the golden tunic, smiling a friendly smile.

"You're back in your own body," Dana said — or was it only her thought, unvoiced?

"No," Aonia replied, and her smile grew wider. "You've lost yours."

"What! What did you say?" Dana's lips formed the words but no sound came out. Yet again her thoughts seemed to have been transferred mentally.

"It was the only way to save you, Dana," Aonia replied.

Dana felt a presence behind her and turned. There stood Kai, a wide smile on his face. "We are together, Dana."

He reached out and took her hand. For the first time since she had known him, she actually felt his fingers close around hers.

"Oh, Kai," she breathed, and put her arms around him. "Kai," she repeated, barely a whisper. She buried her face in his shoulder, feeling, for the first time, the warmth of his skin, the softness of his hair — which tickled her nose. She swallowed as he pressed her closer, when she felt his lips next to her ear and heard his soft breath. Could spirits breathe? Dana did not understand anything, but she clung still more tightly to him, relishing that contact which was so real and so marvelous that her eyes filled with tears. She closed them to experience fully the delicious sensation of Kai's fingers as he combed them through her black hair. Timidly, she lifted her hand to touch his hair, but stopped to stroke the back of his neck. Kai too closed his eyes and sighed as he felt her touch. Dana's fingers brushed his cheek, marveling. Kai opened his eyes, smiled, and lovingly returned her caress. Dana could scarcely breathe, unable to contain the emotion drowning her whole being.

"Kai, this is . . ." was all she could say.

"I know," he replied in a hoarse voice. "I know."

Dana stared into his eyes, and saw in them something that made her uneasy.

"What is it, Kai? What has happened? I don't understand. . . ."

"I wish I didn't have to tell you this," Kai answered, "but I'm afraid that you . . . you are in my world. . . . Dana, you're dead."

A part of Dana was shaken, terrified. But Kai's presence calmed her; at last they were on the same plane. Wasn't that what she had always wanted? "But how . . . ?"

"I was watching you the whole time," said Aonia. "I knew we had to find a place where the Maestro couldn't reach you. And because you are a *Kin-Shannay*, a portal between the worlds of life and death, we spirits could reach into your soul and bring you here. Right now your lifeless body is lying on the floor of the examination room in the Tower, and the Maestro is wondering what happened to his precious slave. I am truly sorry, Dana, but death was the only way to rescue you from his spell."

Dana held on to Kai more tightly. "You have done for me what I would never have dared do by my own hand. At last I am with Kai. I owe you thanks for that," she said.

Kai pulled away and looked into her eyes.

"But it isn't over, Dana. Not for you. You can still go back."

"Go back? What do you mean?"

"We brought you here," said Aonia, "to free you from the enchantment. But it isn't your fate to die now, my young sorcerer. As a *Kin-shannay*, you can still return to the world of the living. It will be as if the spell never happened. And you must return; you must confront the Maestro and eject him from the Tower once and for all."

Dana took a deep breath, or at least it seemed to her she did — she hadn't been aware before of breathing.

"If I go back I'll be separated from Kai again. And I don't want that. There is nothing left for me in the Tower."

"Dana, you must go back," Kai said. His look was urgent, pleading.

"But Kai, we're together at last. Isn't that what you want?"

"There's nothing I want more than to keep you here, Dana. But it can't be, not yet. You have a long life to live. That is what awaits you in the Tower . . . that, and two friends who need your help."

Fenris and Maritta. . . . Dana had forgotten them.

"I understand that it will be a great sacrifice on your part," said Aonia, "because through Kai you have a stronger tie with the world of the spirits than with your own world. But your hour hasn't come. You must return."

"And quickly," Kai urged. "There isn't much time. If you don't go back now, you won't be able to go later. You have only one life, Dana. Don't squander it the way I did."

"You're asking me to give you up."

"Not that, not ever. But everything in its time, and ours hasn't come. Go back to the Tower, Dana. Go back to life. Please."

Dana felt that they were asking too much of her. But it was Kai who was asking, and how could she deny him? She closed her eyes and made an effort to think of Maritta and Fenris, trying to put Kai out of her mind, but the idea of losing him again burned in her like a red-hot sword.

"You will break my heart if you force me to leave," she said.

He tilted his head and smiled at her. "You are strong. And I will see you back there."

Dana sighed. It was true, she was strong. She remembered how she had left her home with the Maestro six years before, convinced that it was the best thing she could do for her family. And now she was supposed to go back because Kai was insisting upon it. When would she be able to think of herself? Well, she imagined that if she went back to the Tower, the Maestro would kill her in battle. So perhaps it didn't make much difference either way. She refused to think about what would happen when she awoke in her body and Kai was again a ghost beyond her reach.

She stepped away from Kai, still holding his hand, and held out the other to Aonia.

"Let's go, Lady of the Tower," she said. "I am going home, and I am going to need your help."

The Maestro had returned to his studio. Fenris was with him, standing guard again at the open window. Soon it would be dawn, and the long, long night would come to an end, but the elf felt no relief at the prospect. He had decided that when the sun rose, he would go somewhere far away from the Tower and let the wolves have their way with the Maestro, even if it meant that on nights of the full moon he himself would undergo the painful transformation into a wolf. It was the least he could do for Dana, whose lifeless body was now lying on the large table of the studio.

At least she and Kai are together now, he told himself, *so perhaps it has been worth it.*

Yet it seemed monstrous to the elf that Dana had died so young. There she lay, cold as stone, her short hair raven-black against the waxen pallor of her face. Her blue eyes, staring vacantly, had lost their gleam of intelligence and serenity. Fenris silently approached the body of his friend and closed her eyelids. His gaze lingered on the red tunic for which she had paid so dearly.

Fenris wept for the first time in his life. Dana had been his one friend, he realized now. He could no longer stay under the same roof with the man who had taken her from him.

He looked at the Maestro, bent over his books.

"I'm leaving," he announced.

"Fine," answered the magician, without turning. "I will expect you tomorrow evening. The moon is still full, I see."

Fenris could not repress the chill those words evoked.

"You're a coward," the Maestro concluded.

"You don't know me as well as you think you do," the elf replied, going back to the window.

And unseen by either of them, Dana opened her eyes. Her heart was beating and she was breathing. This was the second time that she had come back to life, and this time she knew what to expect. Despite a lingering feeling of suffocation, she forced herself not to panic, to focus all her attention on pretending to be dead, on keeping her thought force so quiet that the Maestro would not detect it.

Someone knocked at the door of the studio.

Fenris turned in surprise.

"That miserable dwarf," the sorcerer growled. "I told her never . . ."

"Sorry, sir," came Maritta's voice. "I must come in."

"What do you mean, 'You must come in'? Who do you think you are?" The Maestro waved his hand and the door opened.

Maritta stood there trembling, her eyes wide with fright. "I . . . I've brought you a m-message," she stammered. "A message . . ."

"She's overwrought, poor thing," Fenris said. "Aonia was in her body a long time."

The Maestro sent him a furious glance. "Aonia is dead. And now no one can bring her back to the world of the living. I never want to hear that name again."

"A message . . ." Maritta insisted more firmly.

"Back to the kitchen," the Maestro ordered, "and do not ever disturb me again." He looked down at his books.

Maritta smiled mysteriously. "She said to tell you that you're finished," she declared. "That your hour has come, and that the world of the dead will claim your soul."

Fenris moaned as if he had been punched, and the Maestro turned just in time to see Dana rise from the table with a terrible expression on her face. Her red tunic floated around her and an aureole of golden light issued from her body. Her blue eyes blazed like torches.

"You!" the Maestro gasped. "You were . . . !"

Dana shouted an incantation, and lightning bolts charged with all her accumulated fury shot from her fingertips. In a split second the Maestro raised a barrier of protection, and the bolts bounced off it without reaching him. The sorcerer's lips were mouthing a spell of counterattack when the bloodcurdling howl of a wolf echoed within the stony walls of the Tower. The Maestro looked at Fenris, stunned.

"What . . . ?"

"As Maritta said, your time has come," Fenris told him with a growing smile. "I will protect you no longer."

He went over and stood beside Dana, and together they chanted a new spell, twice as powerful as the first.

With one finger the Maestro traced some magic runes in the air, and instantly an enormous serpent materialized.

"Cretins! Idiots! Infants!" the Maestro spat. "This serpent has fought a thousand battles. You cannot touch me!"

The two friends aimed their bolts at the serpent to no avail. This snake had been invoked by countless magicians before the Maestro summoned it that night. Its fangs distilled poison, and the rattle in its tail struck the floor like a bullwhip. Its hissing filled the room, as it had filled the worst nightmares of the few who had seen it and lived to tell the tale.

Dana and Fenris fought for their lives. The top of the Tower trembled from the force of their attack, but the serpent deflected their rays and shot them back. The few bolts that did strike the creature seemed to have little effect. Dana knew that in a very short time they would run out of ways to contain the monster.

"Mere apprentices! And you think you can get the best of *me*," screamed the Maestro. "You have lost!"

Then, suddenly, his face contracted with pain and he dropped to his knees. The serpent shrank back.

"This . . . can't . . . be," moaned the sorcerer, putting his hand to his side, to a wound gushing blood. The runes he had drawn dissolved in a cloud of fear and pain.

The serpent vanished as rapidly as it had sprung up.

"What happened?" whispered Dana.

"We have a saying in my land," came Maritta's voice. "He who fails to look down will soon be a dead man."

The dwarf stepped from behind the Maestro, holding a bloody dagger.

"No . . ." groaned the magician.

He pushed her aside, lurched toward the door, and staggered down the stairs.

Dana made a move to stop him, but a soft voice restrained her. "Let him go. He is expected."

Dana turned around and saw Kai and Aonia; it was Aonia who had spoken. Bewildered, she looked back toward Maritta.

"Yes," Aonia said. "Yes, it's really Maritta. It was Maritta who stabbed the Maestro."

A terrible scream shook the Tower as the gray wolves raised their howls of triumph.

"The curse has been fulfilled," said Aonia.

Dana was pale. Everything had happened so quickly that she had scarcely had time to absorb it. She went over to Fenris and put her hand on his thin shoulder. "It's over, Fenris," she said softly. "The Maestro is dead. The Tower is ours."

The elf looked at her in confusion. "How did it happen?"

As the first rays of the sun broke through the clouds and shone through the open window, Dana told him of her crossing over, and of her decision to leave Kai and return to the Tower.

"Then the wolves are satisfied," Fenris said when she had finished. "They will go back to the mountains and be like all the other wolves in the valleys of the world."

Dana nodded.

Maritta had been gazing solemnly at Dana. "My Lady of the Tower . . ."

"Yes, Maritta," Dana replied. "She is here with us, and now she can go back to the world of the dead with a tranquil heart. She has had her revenge, and she will rest in peace forever."

Maritta shook her head. An amused look crossed her face. "Come here, my child," she said.

Dana went over to her. "I'm happy you're yourself again," she said, giving the dwarf a hug.

"I have always been myself," said Maritta. "Did you think that Aonia would enter my body without asking my permission? I knew she would be coming back. I have been waiting for her ever since the day she cast her curse on the Valley of the Wolves."

Dana's eyes widened. "So that's why you stayed on in the Tower. Waiting for a chance to . . ."

The dwarf nodded. Her eyes were misty.

Dana felt a spectral touch on her shoulder.

"I must go," said Aonia.

Dana braced herself to say good-bye. The Archmaga, however, was looking meaningfully at Kai.

He straightened, stiff as a rod. "What?" he said. "Is it time already?"

"Your sixteen years are up. She doesn't need you any longer."

Dana suddenly realized what Aonia was saying.

"No, it isn't true! I need him with me. I don't want him to go!" Kai came over and put his hands on her shoulders. "Kai . . ." she pleaded.

He studied every inch of her face, not speaking, losing himself in her gaze.

"I must," was all he said, but it was enough.

"Don't go," she begged, though she knew it was futile. "Don't leave me."

"I'm not leaving you. You are a *Kin-Shannay*, and you know more about life and death than any other mortal. You know that no one ever truly dies, and that I will be waiting for you."

A spark lit Dana's blue eyes.

"In the meanwhile I want you to promise me one thing, and swear by everything holy that you will keep that promise."

"I swear."

Kai's green eyes seemed to hold their old mischief. "Live," he said. "Do not cut your life short in order to meet me before your time. Live a long life, live every moment intensely. Live for me the life I didn't have."

"But . . ."

"You promised," he reminded her. "And now . . . until forever, my love. Thank you for all the years I had with you. Thank you with all my heart."

Kai began to walk away. Dana ran after him.

"Please," Kai said, "your place is here. You must go back to the temple and accept the power the unicorn will give you."

"But what I want . . ."

"I know, and I want it too. But you must be patient and enjoy life, because in all the universe, this life on Earth is unique. Don't do what I did."

Dana's eyes burned into his. "You've been sorry?"

"Every day of my existence on the Other Side. Although sometimes I ask myself whether I would have met you if I hadn't battled that dragon. That I will never know, I suppose." He sighed. "Nor will I ever know whether I killed it. What do you think?"

Dana didn't know whether he was asking her a serious question or simply joking to lighten the tension. "I could find out," she offered.

Kai smiled again and stroked her cheek with his fingertips, and Dana felt his ineffable touch for the last time. Then he turned and walked toward the waiting Aonia.

"Use every bit of what you have learned," Aonia said

to Dana. "With the power you have, and the power the unicorn will give you, you can do great good, *Kin-Shannay.* To start with, you can help that poor elf who suffers so on nights of the full moon."

"Can I really?" asked Dana.

"The magic is in you, and the self-control is in him. He is a Lord of the Wolves. In time he will learn how to use his heritage for his own good and not be a slave to it. But you must guide him."

Dana considered Aonia's words. Fenris was sitting on the floor beside Maritta, watching Dana talk with spirits that he could neither see nor hear. It would be wonderful to do something for him. The prospect of that new challenge cheered her a little.

"Good-bye," said Aonia.

Dana looked at Kai, hoping against hope that he would change his mind, yet knowing that it was not in his power to make that choice. As he gazed back at her with great tenderness, his image grew fainter and fainter until he disappeared.

Dana stood there feeling sad and alone, overcome with emptiness. After a while, she realized that the elf's arm was around her shoulders.

"Has he gone?" Fenris asked softly.

Dana nodded, tears trickling down her cheeks. Fenris led her to the window.

"Look."

The snow-covered landscape shone magnificently beneath the early morning light. Dana saw the mountains, the forest trees; she breathed the crisp clean air. This morning was like many others, yet it was filled with joy and hope.

It was the dawn of a new day in the Valley of the Wolves.

Epilogue

Two men were making slow progress along the valley road. The younger, a redhead with laughing eyes, tugged at the halter of a stubborn mule. Whenever he ceased his efforts, even if only for an instant, the indignant animal balked and refused to move forward again. It obviously considered its load much too heavy for such a long trip.

The older man paused and wiped sweat from his brow. "Is it much farther?" he asked.

"No, just through that stretch of forest ahead, and then we're there," his younger companion answered.

The man raised his eyebrows. "You're not thinking of taking me right up to the Tower, are you?"

The youth whistled and twirled his cap. "How many years since you've been in the valley, my friend? The

Lady of the Tower protects everyone in it. We are all welcome at her hearth."

"Yes, yes, have it your way," the other grumbled. "But I say that place still has a curse on it. Who can trust a magician these days? All you have to do is take a peek at this load we're carrying. . . ."

He fell silent as he spied two figures on horseback at the top of the hill. Both wore capes that fluttered behind them in the wind.

"By all that's holy . . ." murmured the man.

The redhead pulled at the mule's halter and sweated and strained his way up the hill. The old man followed, a skeptical expression on his face.

The first rider threw back the hood of her cape. The last rays of the setting sun caught the features of a beautiful young woman with long hair, black as a raven's wing, and blue eyes as deep and serene as the calmest sea.

Approaching her, the redheaded youth bowed. "G-g-good afternoon, Lady," he stammered, transfixed by the intensity of her eyes. "We brought you . . ."

"Thank you, Nicolás." She glanced toward the hooded figure next to her on a chestnut stallion, and then back to the two travelers. "May I see it?"

"Of course!" Nicolás touched two fingers to his cap and waited for the old man to say or do something. But his companion seemed unable to move, so he gave him a little push. Between them, they unloaded the stubborn mule and laid an enormous bundle before the Lady.

The old man got his tongue back. "We had to look a long time before we found it," he told her.

She nodded. "I'm not surprised. Your efforts will be rewarded."

The youth and the old man set about unwrapping the bundle. The sun was sinking behind the mountains when the contents were finally laid bare.

The bones before the sorcerer would not yield a complete skeleton. Even so, she could tell that it had been a medium-size dragon.

"We knew it was a blue one," the old man explained, pointing to the skull. "You see, only blue dragons have horns like these. As for the ribs . . ."

"Did you find the other object?" A melodious voice came from the depths of the second rider's hood. "The Lady doesn't have all day."

The Lady of the Tower calmed him with a wave of her hand.

The old man looked at the Lady, freshly impressed. "Y-yes, your honors," he stuttered. He pulled an object from his pouch and handed it to the woman with a little bow.

She unwrapped it with meticulous care and examined the object in the last light of day. It was an ancient dagger. Not a precious one — there were no jewels on the hilt, no silver filigree on the blade. It was just a very old, everyday knife, rusted and useless.

The sorcerer, however, closed her eyes and kissed the

hilt tenderly. Then she lovingly rewrapped it and slid it into a pouch at her waist.

"Where did you find it?" she asked.

"It was lying among the dragon's ribs, my Lady," the man replied.

"Do you think it could have killed the dragon? It's rather small."

"I can't really say . . . but perhaps so. The jawbone is shattered. See? Maybe the knife — maybe for some reason the beast dropped out of the sky and cracked its head on the rocks."

The Lady of the Tower observed the dragon's skull with interest.

"At any rate, it all happened a long time ago," the man added, wagging his head. "Centuries, probably. Who can know?"

"I know," was all she said in her gentle voice.

"Ah, well, then. You say so . . . it's bound to be true."

The Lady nodded. "You have carried out your charge," she said. "Now I will fulfill my part of the bargain."

As the man stepped forward, he found that a bulging sack had appeared in his hands. He jumped back and looked at it with suspicion.

"Don't worry, it won't disappear," the Lady assured him. Her companion gave an amused laugh.

"Do you need us to help you carry this back to the Tower?" Nicolás asked, pointing to the dragon's skeleton.

"No, Nicolás. Thank you. You may go now."

Again the youth touched his fingers to his cap and tugged at the mule, which was considerably more cooperative now that it was free of its load. The older man followed, clutching the sack of money tightly to his chest and casting one last wary glance at the figures on horseback.

The Lady and her companion remained a while. When a mantle of stars had spread across the valley, the Lady looked up. The moon was in the first quarter — a crescent moon — and between the points of the crescent shone an exceptionally beautiful star.

The second rider pulled back the hood of his cape and let moonlight fall upon his gentle elfin features. Then he tipped his head back and howled.

It was a long, drawn-out sound, and it was answered from the mountains where brother wolves chorused their greeting.

The Lady of the Tower looked at the elf and smiled. Beneath a starry sky they slowly rode back toward the Tower, leaving behind the pale bones of the blue dragon bathed in the light of the waxing moon.

This translation was edited by Cheryl Klein and Donna Brooks and art directed by Elizabeth Parisi. The text was set in Jansen, with chapter titles and numbers in Rapture Heavenly. This book was printed and bound by Berryville Graphics in Virginia. The manufacturing was supervised by Jaime Capifali.